TWISTED TIMELINES

STEFON MEARS

Also by Stefon Mears

Cavan Oltblood Series
Half a Wizard
The Ice Dagger
Spells of Undeath

Spells for Hire
Devil's Shoestring
Zombie Powder
Spirit Trap
Dragon's Blood

The Rise of Magic
Magician's Choice
Sleight of Mind
Lunar Alchemy
Three Fae Monte
The Sphinx Principle
Double Backed Magic

The Telepath Trilogy
Surviving Telepathy
Immoral Telepathy
Targeting Telepathy

Edge of Humanity
Caught Between Monsters
Hunting Monsters

Power City Tales
Not Quite Bulletproof
No Money in Heroism

Sects and the City
Prince of a Thousand Worlds
Longhairs and Short Tales: A Collection of Cat Stories
Devil's Night
Portal-Land, Oregon
Stealing from Pirates
Fade to Gold
With a Broken Sword
Twice Against the Dragon
The House on Cedar Street
Sudden Death
On the Edge of Faerie
Confronting Legends (Spells & Swords Vol. 1)
Uncle Stone Teeth and Other Macabre Poems
The Patreon Collection, Vol. 1-5 (Vol. 6, coming soon)
The 30-Day Novel and Beyond!

Published by Thousand Faces Publishing, Portland, Oregon

http://1kfaces.com

Front cover image © Rolffimages | Dreamstime.com (File ID: 172024287)

"The Face of Trouble" and "Forty Years Among the Elves" were originally published in *The Patreon Collection, Volume 1*

"Paradox. Lost." was originally published in *Fiction River: Visions of the Apocalypse,* from WMG Publishing, July 2016

ISBN: 978-1-948490-23-8

TWISTED TIMELINES

CONTENTS

FOREWORD

Growing up, I didn't care for time travel stories. I never really got into *Dr. Who*, and the time travel episodes of *Star Trek* were pretty much always my least favorite.

Kind of weird, when I think about it. I didn't mind them going to worlds that emulated, say 1920s gangsters, but if they went to the 1920s, I lost interest.

Then, when I was in my late teens, a movie came out that changed my mind about time travel. *Bill and Ted's Excellent Adventure.* It was goofy. It made fun of itself, even as it was telling its story. They played games with time travel, even as they used it.

But it worked. For me, at least. Your mileage, as they say, may vary.

But it got me thinking that if they could have fun with time travel, then so could I. And that's what I did with the stories in this collection. I just let myself have fun, and write all kinds of stories, from the adventurous to the silly to the dramatic to the bizarre.

Some of the characters in this story travel time deliberately, some are yanked through time, and at least one may not have traveled at all. A couple of others find themselves outside of time, and have to get back.

So sit back and enjoy.

Oh, and be excellent to each other. And party on, dudes!

THE FACE OF TROUBLE

THE FACE OF TROUBLE

I never know which face is mine.

In the crowd. In the mirror. I could be any of them. I could be you. And I might never know it.

I wake in the morning. Already a change. Last I recall I was a hospital orderly working the night shift in Nineteen Eighty-Six. I was a big guy then. Hefty, but with at least as much muscle as fat. But it's morning this time, yellow sun high over the fir trees and snowy mountain peaks outside my cabin window.

The glass looks either cheap or old, little runnels of warp here and there.

Did I go backward again? No. I hear a heater click on, smell warmed dust entering the room. The window is caulked around the edges. The "log" cabin around me is façade.

The girl in the bed is real. Leggy. Dark skinned like me. Blonde. Probably not like me. Rare for this skin tone. She's still asleep, sprawled in a silk nightdress and a mess of plaid flannel sheets. For some reason I don't think she picked them out.

Did I?

I'm male this time, a wiry kind of skinny. And unlike the blonde, I sleep in the nude. Or at least I did last night. I dig through the chest of drawers (also faux log design) but no sign of a wallet. Not on the tree stump nightstand either. But I do find underwear, jeans and a plain white tee shirt that fit me. Plus some silkier underwear and shapelier clothes that probably fit her.

Frankly, I'd rather wear those. Men's clothing is so plain and stolid. Boring. But my body is male again and I need to blend in.

The girl is good and bad news. Good because we're obviously a couple. Neither of us cheating. Well, I suppose this could be a weekend away from our spouses or something, but at least neither of us is wearing a wedding ring. So *probably* not cheating.

That's good. A couple of wake-ups ago I found out I was cheating on my husband because he walked in at, shall we say, an inopportune moment?

Hard to apologize when you don't know the person yelling at you. Which is the bad part about the blonde. She's going to expect me to know who she is, and where we are, and probably what our plans are for the day. You know, the typical things that most people take for granted. The kinds of things I never know.

Like my face. I could go look in the mirror above the dresser right now, if I wanted, but it wouldn't do me any good. All I would see is my mission. And I'm not ready for that yet. Damn it, this time I want to get my legs under me *before* people start shooting at me.

Doesn't seem like a lot to ask, but you'd be surprised how rarely it works out that way.

I finally find my wallet and a room key in a light, tan jacket, hanging on a wire hook in a small armoire. Must be summer in the mountains, because even the purple jacket next to mine is light. Two small roller suitcases on the floor, next to hiking boots and tennis shoes. Guess that tells me what the plan is for today.

Good way to spend a vacation. Wonder if I'll ever get to find out.

Colorado driver's license says my name is Jason Ogilvie. It's got a birth date too, but that doesn't do me much good when I don't know what year it is. I do know that this guy was born after the last time I woke up. Which tells me nothing, really, but I always check.

You might think I could see my face in the driver's license picture. Doesn't work that way. I don't see my mission, because the surface isn't reflective, but all I do see where the face should be is what I call the "Traveler haze." Like a cloud of green gas around the head of the host.

There's cash in the wallet too, and two types of credit cards. Seems Mr. Ogilvie does pretty well for himself. He also carries a gym card and a couple of others with store names on them, but they don't look like credit cards. Nothing that tells me who Mr. Ogilvie is. What he does. What his hobbies are.

Well, Mr. Ogilvie, I'll try to get your body back to you in one piece. If it works that way. I don't know what happens to the people who host me, after I leave.

"Come back to bed, Jason." The blonde's voice is smooth, sultry. "It's too early for breakfast."

"Be there in a second." I pull on the sneakers and turn toward the front door. "I just want to pick up a paper."

"Come on, Baby." The words sound taunting more that teasing. They're followed by a distinctive click. The hammer pulled back on a pistol. "I insist."

I close my eyes and curse whatever fates managed to arrange this arrival. I open my eyes before I turn around, but I might as well not have bothered. I already know what I'm going to see, and I'm not disappointed.

The blonde is sitting up in bed, holding a forty-four caliber revolver in a steady, two-handed grip. Physically she looks fetching, like the cover of some old detective pulp. I got to read dozens of those on one long assignment. She's even got a sinful smile going.

But none of that is the problem. The problem is the green haze of a Traveler I can see surrounding her head. The same way, no doubt, she can see it around mine. I can make out the smile, but that's about it.

"Should have checked the mirror," says the blonde. "Now you'll die without even knowing your mission. Talk about a black mark on your record."

"You could let me check now." You could let me get next to that window too. "Just because we're on opposite sides doesn't mean--"

"Yes it does."

She pulls the trigger.

I DIVE FOR THE DOOR. TOO SLOW. THE ROAR SLAMS MY EARDRUMS. Bullet hits my shoulder like a meteorite. Spins me around. I hit the door jaw first, slide to the floor.

She's on her feet now. Setting for another shot.

Still holding my wallet. I throw it at her face. Scramble out the door into a disaster: crowd. People pour into the light wooden hall, not all of them dressed. Screaming. Shouting. Looking everywhere. Pointing at me.

I push through them. Good hand first. My shoulder on fire, each stiff-arm to clear my path gets me flares of pain.

I run down a wide sweep of stairs, carpeted now. More loud confusion. People with nametags trying to get control. Parents wrestling with children. Angry faces. Scared faces. Crying faces. But I'm the one with napalm in his shoulder.

Must be why I'm crying too.

Instinct screams at me to run and hide. Get out of the building and find a private place to deal with the wound and find out what the hell I'm doing here. But that's the wrong play. Blondie will be waiting outside. She didn't chase me, so she must have gone out the window. No crowd that way. No questions.

It's what I would have done.

She's got a gun and information. I don't even have a wallet.

I let some bald, obese manager lead me into a quiet room with a couch. The room smells like burnt coffee. I sit, trying not to jostle my arm while he hovers, bouncing foot to foot like he's going to spring into action anytime now. I have my doubts. He's sweating like this is the most action he's seen in a year, maybe longer. He's talking, but he's not saying anything worth hearing.

Looks like a break room, now that I can look around. Round Formica table with cheap plastic chairs, refrigerator in the corner, coffee pot, and ... is that a microwave? I think so. They've gotten small since my last wake-up.

Sitting still calls my attention to the lesser of my wounds: my jaw. Must have banged it pretty good on that door, because I can feel it now despite the burning pain from my left shoulder. I probably wrenched poor Jason's back when I fell, too, which means it's going to stiffen up the longer I'm sitting.

I have to get out of here.

The manager keeps chattering away, so I sigh and tune in, trying to ignore my pulsing pains, the blood all over my hands and arm and sticking my white shirt to my side.

"...because if this is a drug thing I demand that you let me know right now."

"Wait, what? Drugs?" Is this guy serious?

Apparently.

"I've already called nine-one-one, and they're sending the police as well as an ambulance. But I'm warning you right now, if this is about drugs or gangs--"

"Drugs? Gangs?" I say. "What, because I'm black?"

That pokes a hole in him. He tries straightening his atrocious tie, and that seems to give him back some of his courage, even if he looks sweatier and clammier than I am.

"I'm just saying that guests at Pinewood do not shoot one another. And that if you're involved in something illegal--"

"DO YOU HAVE ANY ASPIRIN?"

Fat boy seems to remember I'm hurt and his bravado crumbles. "I'm so sorry. Of course. You're the victim here. Just let me..."

He scurries out of the room and I lock the door behind him, my back complaining now with each step. Idiot probably thought of his private stash of aspirin in his desk drawer or something, and forgot that hotel will likely have some in a central location. Like, say, the break room. Not that I need the aspirin anyway. What I need is a few minutes to myself.

I lean back on the couch. My back and jaw are easy enough to ignore right now, so I focus on the pain in my shoulder. Really get to know its character: hot, yes, but with an icy interior, pulsing, ever pulsing with each beat of my speeding heart.

But I can slow my heartbeat down. Oh, yes. Slow it from a race with just a little more focus and intention, just a chance for my breaths to get deeper. Almost like every breath is pulling in from somewhere way deep in my torso, and slithering back out past the pain, isolating the pain, sectioning it off behind a wall where it can't touch me.

My jaw unclenches. I hadn't even realized I'd tightened it. That pain is gone too, but that doesn't matter right now. Someone's knocking on the door, but I don't care. I just need to relax further, feel my arm and leg muscles grow slack, my neck and shoulder muscles grow limp, every inch of muscle in my body slowing down and easing to a nice relaxed state.

Pounding on the door now. Pounding like my heart was doing less than a minute ago. But not my heart. Mr. Jason Ogilvie's heart. Sorry, Jason. I can't do anything about that shoulder. Or your back. Or your jaw.

I feel worst about your shoulder. But help is on the way, and the bullet mostly grazed the muscle. It'll hurt like hell for a while, and it will scar, but it won't do any long term damage to you... You'll ... be just fine ... at the gym ... and I'll find another ... host....

I hear a key in the lock. I open my eyes.

I'm still in the break room. The manager throws the door open, framed in the doorway like some cartoon. Behind him I can see more people in nametags. Two guys in badges, too, and tan uniforms.

And I'm still stuck in the body of Mr. Jason Ogilvie.

GREAT. I STILL DON'T KNOW WHAT'S GOING ON AND THE COPS ARE HERE. And me, covered in blood, lying on a couch in a room with the only exit blocked by anxious hotel workers. My deep state of mind is blown, but at least my shoulder's stopped hurting.

Wait. My shoulder doesn't hurt? That pain should have come roaring back by now. And my jaw. And my back...

"Why was that door locked?" barks the manager. Seems that having cops at his back makes him feel all tough and official.

"Because I hoped for a couple of minutes without more racist assumptions." I let the words slur a little, like my wound is getting to me. The cops, both trim, clean-shaven types, push past Fat Boy, giving him accusatory glares as they pass.

"We'll take it from here," says the first cop, one hand encouraging the manager to leave and the other ready to close the door behind him. "Send in the paramedics as soon as they arrive."

"I'm Officer Gutierrez," says the other one to me. "My partner is Officer Jones." He looks me over with sympathetic eyes while his partner brings me aspirin and a glass of water.

I don't need the aspirin anymore, which worries me, but I have to play it off. Toss the bitter pills in my mouth. Shaky hand on the glass. That kind of thing. They give me room to swallow, Jones talking softly into his radio while Gutierrez writes in a notepad, looking around like the break room details matter to him.

Under the pretext of grabbing my shoulder, I let my finger prod the skin. Clean. Perfect. Not the skin of a man reporting his gunshot wound to the police.

Never had a wound heal before. But then I've never failed to dump a host before either. Did those bastards upgrade the tech and not tell me?

Word to the wise: never take a job involving time travel. No matter how much you need the money.

"So," said Officer Gutierrez, apparently having given me all the space I'm going to get, "the paramedics are two minutes from here, but your shooter is still out there. Who shot you? Why? The more you tell us right now, the more we can help you."

I so want to turn in the blonde. But I now have less than two minutes before medical professionals start asking why there's a bullet hole in my bloody shirt, but no wound in my shoulder.

I clutch one hand to my mouth and burp out the word, "Bathroom!" I lurch to my feet and stumble for the door.

"Use the sink," tries Gutierrez, but Jones has already opened the door for me. The manager and two of his cronies are waiting like they've got a turn for interrogation coming.

"Bathroom!" I burp again, and they part before me as I push past them. Damn near lose my footing, but it makes my stumbling walk more convincing. I hear footsteps behind me. Probably Officer Gutierrez, angry that I've left his controlled environment.

The bathroom is the small, stall-less kind. Locking door (thank God!), soapy air freshener, a toilet and a urinal. Floor sparkles like it's never been soiled. One small window high above the toilet. I fake-cough a few times, painfully aware that I have no ready quantity of liquid to toss into the toilet for verisimilitude.

I don't care anyway. The mirror above the sink is all that matters.

I look in the mirror and see the reflection of the bathroom around me. And in the center, I see a blacked out humanoid shape, with white text scrolling slowly up from the bottom: "You will go to the hotel restaurant in six hours, twenty-two minutes, thirty eight seconds." That time continues to count down as I read. "You will hear a girl child start crying. When she does you are to say to her, GOTTA LEARN TO SOLVE YOUR OWN PROBLEMS, KID. You will memorize that exact phrase and repeat it without deviation. You will retain your current host until you do. – the Management."

Seriously? That's why I'm here? Some sage wisdom at a "random" moment that will play a key role in some important person's development?

I'm not kidding. If anyone ever offers you a job that involves time travel, just say no. Not even once.

Anyway, the blonde may not have killed me with that gunshot, but she screwed me. There's no way I can just walk into the restaurant tonight and speak my piece like Johnny Normal. Not with cops breathing down my neck and the whole hotel terrified at the sight of me.

I look at the mirror again, hoping for an update. The only thing different is the time, which keeps up its steady countdown.

A polite fist knocks five times on the door. Officer Gutierrez's voice follows.

"Mr. Ogilvie? If you're finished, we still need answers to those questions, and the paramedics are here to tend to your shoulder." Trying to sound supportive. Like a friend. But I can hear the note of suspicion in his voice.

I'm not acting like a gunshot victim. And he knows it.

I look up at that small window above the toilet. Good thing you're a skinny boy, Jason Ogilvie.

By the time that polite fist gets more urgent on the door I'm halfway out the window and psyching myself up for the six-foot drop. I land pretty good for a fugitive. Which is what I am now.

Never thought I'd wish I had a gunshot wound back. Freaking management probably think they're doing me a favor.

Anyway, I'm on a dirt trail now, just outside the faux-log-cabin exterior. Apparently the whole hotel follows that motif, as though they used to make log cabins three stories tall. Lots of bushes and evergreens, so I head straight into them, praying I don't catch myself on some kind of stinging nettle or poison oak or something equally offensive.

But I'm not a woodsman. My steps are heavy with the need to put distance between myself and a bunch of questions I can't answer and a cell I don't have time for. I break twigs and leaves with abandon, surprise a raccoon, and try to tell myself that the dozens of birdsongs all around me down out my ruckus.

But I know that's a lie.

So I rush, and hope that by the time they can begin to follow I'll have slowed down and doubled-back a few times, anything I can think of to throw them off the trail.

Somewhere out here is the blonde. And though the cops are after her too, in theory, I know she's already holed up somewhere. Probably threw her off by going out the side the way I did. She was probably watching the front, and by the time she realizes I went a different way, she'll have to contend with the cops. So I did myself that much good at least.

Except that she doesn't need to hunt me.

That thought stops me, makes me lean against a redwood tree and take a break while I get my breath back. The air is clean. Crisp. I'd probably find it refreshing under other circumstances. But right now the air is only good for the oxygen it gives me.

No sounds of pursuit yet. That's good. But that doesn't help my mission. The blonde may not know what I'm supposed to do in that restaurant tonight, but I'd bet my bloody tee-shirt she knows where and when it will go down. All she has to do is hide herself away and wait for me.

She won't even have to shoot me. All she'll have to do is point and scream. The crowd will do the rest.

I have to take her out.

God, I hate this job.

I can't say there's anything I particularly enjoy about time travel. I mean, the novelty of the new eras and sights pales pretty quickly with the realization that you're never comfortable with the technology. It's never more advanced than I know how to use, but adapting to the local limitations takes time and can make you look like the one dunce who never learned how to use something everyone else takes for granted. Plus, you have to keep your mouth shut about tech, or you'll end up asking about something they don't have yet. God only knows what that would do.

But there's nothing I hate more than killing for this job. The management decides what I'm doing with each wake-up, and they make it clear that my task is *the most important thing in the world*. It's worth dying for. It's worth killing for. They may even be right. For all I know, that little girl is going to grow up to be some world-changing scientist or politician. Whatever she becomes must be a big deal. I mean, someone sent another Traveler back to stop me, and that one went straight to lethal force.

But it's not the Traveler that bugs me so much as the host. I can't kill the Traveler without killing the host.

And that's not right, damn it.

It's not right that Jason Ogilvie has to either die or go up on a murder charge for the sake of my sacred fucking mission. It's not right that the same is true for his girlfriend. These are human beings, with friends. Family. Lives. Futures of their own.

But not anymore. Those lives and futures just got bartered away for someone else's. Someone the management considers more important. And those lives are shot all because that blonde pulled a trigger.

No.

All because they were unlucky enough to be hosts.

But letting my mind linger on this isn't going to help me any. If I don't complete my mission, then two lives have been ruined for nothing. And that's not acceptable.

Time for the hunted to become the hunter.

But first, I wait.

The sun is high, but not yet at its apex, so it's late morning. Not more than an hour has passed since I read my assignment, so I've got about five hours and some change before the big moment. At least Jason Ogilvie must be used to colder temperatures, because the slight nip in the air isn't bothering me.

If cops call in a manhunt they'll catch me. No doubt they've got some hunters and I've left a trail a mile wide. I'm sure of it, but I admit I can't tell. I look back now and don't see any signs of my passing. I've been trying to stay quiet and careful after that initial burst of distance. Looks like I've done a pretty good job. No snapped twigs or bent bushes that I can see. No obvious footprints, or line of crushed leaves. Nothing that would tell me that someone came this way

But I'm not the one I have to fool.

All right. What do I know? Jason's girlfriend is playing host to a Traveler, with orders to stop me. Did the girlfriend already have a gun? Or has her Traveler been here long enough to acquire it?

Wait. Back in the chest of drawers I saw three more pairs of underwear next to three more pairs of socks (well, two each now that I was dressed), and the bottom drawer had two pairs of underwear that had been flung in, not stacked, along with two pairs of loose socks: dirty clothes. This was day three of a five day trip. Maybe four days, with a spare set of clothes in case of ... oh, let's just say blood stains.

Could I have gotten hold of a handgun in two days? Maybe. In the right place. In the right time. But that looked like a big gun in the blonde's hands. Not the sort of gun that would go with the clothes I saw in her side of the dresser, much less the clutch purse hanging in the armoire.

So either the gun is Jason's or the Traveler picked it up. I check Jason's hands over: some callousing on the palm near the index finger. Just the place that forty-four might rub when fired. Probably Jason's gun then. I pull the bloody tee-shirt free from my host's chest and try to spot any tattoos. None.

Not in a gang then, probably. And the wallet had no police I.D., so either Jason is a Fed or a gun enthusiast or both. Doesn't really matter, except that his shooting reflexes are likely to be good if I get his hands on a gun.

But I don't have one right now. And the Blonde does.

Police and paramedics got here fast. That means that despite the rustic look of the hotel, we can't be far from civilization. Still, all I've seen during my escape has been forest and mountain, so likely there's only one reliable way up and down to civilization. And the police know I'm out here in my sneakers, with no jacket and no wallet, and a gunshot wound in my shoulder.

They don't need to hunt me. They know I can't get far. So no manhunt then.

Well, maybe a hunt for Blondie, since Officers Gutierrez and Jones know I'm not carrying a pistol and everyone and their brother had to have heard the gunshot. Whether they see me as an innocent who panicked and ran or a guy who's guilty of something else, they know I'm not the shooter. Only one other occupant in the room, and if she went out the window the way I think she did, she left a trail. At least at first.

So. The police are probably looking for Blondie – and halfheartedly looking for me – and Blondie knows she has a good five hours before I make my move.

She's likely to be worried about the locals. Not about me.

Good.

JUST CIRCLING THE HOTEL TAKES ME A COUPLE OF HOURS. I FIRST TRIED to start from where I was, but I'd doubled-back and drifted off of point enough times that I was pretty well lost, even though I didn't know it.

Did I mention that I'm not a woodsman?

So I had to waste some time finding my way back toward the hotel first, but it was big enough and central enough that I didn't have to get into sight of it to know where I was. Then I was able to sidle my way around from the back, where I started, to the far side from my ignominious exit.

Right now I'm tucked in the low branches of an oak tree, irritating more than a few squirrels if their barking is any indication. Moved a few birds too. But from here I can see the kitchen door. I've already seen some guy in white clothes and an apron carry out three loads of rubbish for the Dumpster a few feet from the swinging door.

Two young cops walked past a few minutes ago. If they gave the area more than a cursory check, I couldn't tell.

A couple of old compact cars are parked on worn grass in the sixty feet or so of open space between the hotel and the start of the woods. I'm about twenty feet further into those woods and grateful for the seat.

I can smell grilled cheese, and my stomach reminds me frequently that Jason Ogilvie has not eaten anytime recently. Well, I'm sorry about that, Jason. Today you're fasting.

I would love a glass of water though.

No time to think about...

Wait. I'm calm, or at least as calm as I'm going to get right now. I'm alone. Maybe I can't jump hosts on this assignment, but maybe I can do more than heal my aches and pains.

I ease back against the rough trunk of the oak and begin. The slower heartbeat. The deeper breathing. All the little tricks that slide my mind to the point of disconnection from the body of Jason Ogilvie, even though I can't push past that point. I can feel the tether now, like a piece of psychic elastic tying me to the body.

Last time I pushed at the tether, felt a snap and assumed I was snapping back into a new host. So I push at it again. Snap. And again. Snap. And again!

SNAP!

My eyes blink open.

I'm still in the body of Jason Ogilvie, still on the branch of the oak tree, and still waiting for the blonde to take up her position in the kind of place I would choose for an ambush. In fact, I don't think anything's changed. Even my tee shirt is still bloody and, let's be honest, smelly.

Wait. I'm not hungry anymore. Or thirsty. Or even tired. Not *that* has possibilities. If only the gig were in the morning instead of this afternoon, I might be able to use that little trick to give me an edge on Blondie, say around two in the morning.

Oh, well. At least I'll be fresh when we face off.

I'm in the right place. I'm sure of it. Good view of the hotel and the outside door closest to the restaurant. I can even see into the parking lot if I crane my head just right, but I don't need to do that.

I'm right above the cleanest vantage point for an armed person expecting to see someone try to sneak in the back door.

Based on the sun's position, I'd say I have about three hours before this is all due to go down. Blondie will probably get here in two.

All I have to do now is wait.

COULDN'T BE MORE THAN THIRTY MINUTES LATER WHEN BLONDIE strolls up from the parking lot. Traveler haze around her head and a casual, barefoot saunter like she doesn't have a care in the world. Pistol in one hand, can of gasoline in the other. The kind you might see attached to the back of a Jeep.

How did she get past the police carrying a pistol? What is she doing with that...

No.

Oh, no.

I scramble down the oak as fast as I can, jumping the last six feet or so. Rough landing this time. Twist my ankle. Cry out before I can stop myself.

She sees me.

I freeze, hands and one knee on the ground. I want to dive behind the oak but my arms won't cooperate.

Blondie raises her gun hand...

...and waves?

No fast draw. No hail of bullets. She just raises her gun hand and gives me this little twisty wave like she's the Queen of England or something. If the Queen of England waved with a forty-four. She turns and heads for the kitchen door.

In motion now I scrabble forward. Push up with my hands until my feet manage to hold me. My left ankle bitches as I rush at a limping lurch.

Blondie raises the gun. Hesitates. Must know that if she misses she calls the cops down on top of her.

The back door opens. Young white trash guy in white. Turns whiter than his clothes when he sees the gun. Screams.

I'm past the trees now, closing at a mad hobble.

Blondie pistol-whips White Trash. He falls back against the door frame, face bloody. Twisting away from her raised forty-four.

Burly guy in the doorway now. Stained kitchen whites. Mustaches down past his chin, gray as his hair.

Blondie's shin finds his Special Place, turns his face red and sinks him like a lead weight.

I'm halfway across the open area now. Cops running in from the parking lot. Some idiot rookie with his gun drawn. Couple of vets behind him – Gutierrez one of them – yelling for everyone to hit the ground.

I dive. Eat grass and oily dirt.

Blondie opens fire.

I cover my head. Shots. So many gunshots. Each one a sledge-hammer on my eardrums.

Screams.

Chaos.

I hate time travel.

IT'S LATER NOW. I'M STILL IN HANDCUFFS, THOUGH EVEN GUTIERREZ admits he can't prove I've done anything wrong. Threatens to keep poor Jason Ogilvie overnight anyway. On suspicion. Or something. That part isn't really clear to me. But apparently he has that power.

So I sit here in the back of an open ambulance with Officer Jones babysitting me. Every so often he asks why I ran. Oh, he phrases it differently each time, like telling me they would have protected me, or how they would have caught Sara – the name of Blondie's poor host, who will be spending more than a single night in jail at the very least, after she comes out of intensive care – before any of this badness went down yadda yadda.

I just shrug each time. I've got nothing to say that he'll understand anyway.

I don't even know why I'm sitting in the back of the ambulance. They probably hope I'll talk if they don't throw me in the back of a squad car. The paramedics couldn't find anything wrong, after they wrapped my ankle. They asked a few times about the bullet hole and the blood.

I just shrug at them too. Truth is I haven't said a word. Let them blame that on shock.

At least half the guests are out here, milling about the parking lot. I think the police are checking the hotel for other possible "explosive devices."

I'm just about to hold up my handcuffs again, trying to ask without words if Jones will take them off, when Gutierrez comes jogging up, one hand holding his tan hat and the other securing his firearm.

"Why the kitchen?" he says as soon as he comes to a stop.

I look up at him. My face is blank, as far as I can tell.

"Still not talking, huh? You know this isn't helping you look innocent in all this."

I blink.

"Fine. I want you to come take a look at something. Then you see if you find your tongue." He hauls me up by my shoulder. I notice his baton/gun hand is free, just in case. "See if you still want to protect your girlfriend."

I just shake my head, slow and sad, like I'm trying to say he's got it all wrong. Which he does. Not that I can explain. I let him drag me past the gawkers, Jones on our tail. Gutierrez pushes us past the front door and into the lobby. More gawkers sweating the action, but some people just going about their day.

Maybe they aren't checking for more explosives. Maybe people are just watching for the same reason they rubberneck at accidents.

Anyway, the manager and his two remoras fall into step, babbling something about the damage to the kitchen and who is going to pay for it. Gutierrez doesn't answer. Jones follows his lead.

Me, I've started watching the crowd while they drag me past the staircase.

And into the restaurant.

There she is. A little girl crying at a table over by the kitchen door. Mother crouched down trying to hush her. Father sitting at the table, adjusting his napkin as though the whole scene is beneath him.

Gutierrez drags me closer, aiming for the kitchen door. Five steps away now.

My heartbeat kicks into overdrive. My breaths pant. Gutierrez raises an eyebrow, like he's discovered something. Like he thinks I know what's in the kitchen. Three steps.

"You know, don't you, you bastard," says Gutierrez. Two steps. "You're responsible."

"Hey!" I yell to get the family's attention.

Gutierrez yanks me, trying to speed me past them, but I dig in my heels. My ankle screams in protest.

Then the girl looks at me.

"Gotta learn to solve your own problems, kid."

SNAP goes the tether, yanking me out of the body of Jason Ogilvie. I never have a chance to see the girl react. To know if she understands my words, let alone my message.

I never have a chance to get poor Jason Ogilvie and his girlfriend out of their tight spot.

But right now I'm nowhere. Outside of space. Outside of time. This whole gig was only supposed to last an hour, my time. I've already done at least three years of work, relative time.

I hope my hour is up soon. I can't stomach this job much longer.

I'm telling you. Never take a job in time travel.

<<<<>>>>

FORTY YEARS AMONG
THE ELVES

FORTY YEARS AMONG THE ELVES

Highway rest stops deserve their bad reputation, but not for the reason everything thinks. They aren't full of drug dealers or serial killers waiting to slit your throat from the backseat. And they aren't havens for gay sex, though I wish they were. I could have used a no-strings lay that night. It would have been much better than what I found.

I was in the thirtieth hour of a forty-five hour road trip down the west coast from Alaska. Just me in my beat-up Dodge pickup. A truck old enough to rattle and bitch if the speedometer crept over sixty-five, but at least it smelled good. Like fresh dirt and verbena. The dirt was all over the cracked vinyl seats, mostly. Well, it was also on the dashboard. And the stained floor mats, but it was hard to spot there under the legacy of pine needles, fir needles, and mud.

Jace hated the dirt in my truck. I heard about it every time I drove us someplace. "It's not like you don't own a vacuum, Lex. The least you could do is use it." That dirt was probably the beginning of the end for us. Jace was the kind of guy who worried about getting his precious pants dirty. I was the kind of guy who didn't always remember to bring his sleeping bag when he went camping.

That was why the spontaneous road trip. I walked in on Jace with

Mark. Tall like me. Blonde like me. Clean — not at all like me. I bet Mark never even *has* to clean dirt out from under his fingernails, much less forgets to.

I didn't say anything. Just grabbed my go-bag and threw into it the half-dozen things I kept at Jace's place. Jace was saying something, but I didn't hear him. I kept hearing my mother's voice, telling me that Jace looked like a player. Didn't look like a boy to settle down with.

I should have listened.

Anyway, I could have just gone home, but that was not going to happen. Sometimes I just need to drive. Made the Dodge perfect up in Alaska, where the roads have as many dings and nicks as my truck's fenders. Half an hour any drivable direction from Juneau and I could count on not having strangers getting in my face with their needs. Just me time among the giant trees and deep, deep skies.

But this time I stayed on the freeway. I was just so mad at Jace I couldn't stand being in the same state as him. I got fixated on visiting my mom all the way down in Eugene, Oregon, and just making it in one long drive.

Yeah, I know it's stupid. I wasn't in a good place.

I did nap once in a Tim Horton's parking lot somewhere around Prince Rupert, British Columbia, but it wasn't worth much. I think the coffee did me more good than the twenty restless minutes with my feet on the bench seat. That and driving with the windows down. Nothing like fresh, cold November air on your face to keep you awake. Especially when it has the wonderful smell of acres of evergreens.

I was dressed for that kind of cold, too. Long Johns under my jeans and flannel, plus a good winter jacket in the cab with me, in case of another unexpected snow.

But somewhere around hour thirty my little wakey-wakey tricks started failing me. I didn't mind the yawning so much. It was the third time I caught my head nodding forward that scared me. That and the sickly horn of a little Geo something that objected to my drifting into his lane.

That was when I decided to park at the next rest stop and sleep.

Twenty minutes later, I pulled into the sort of place that could have served as a horror movie set. I even went through a wave of mist when I pulled off the freeway. Decrepit public restroom building complete with broken windows over metal grating, graffiti about blood and death, and a suspicious hole in the roof. Three dozen parking spaces, all empty except one down all the way at the far end where a semi cab without a trailer rusted away at the fenders.

I wasn't going to go close enough to check, but a glance made me think that semi had been parked there since the nineties. Something about the awful teal paint job.

I just pulled into a worn spot down at the other end, as far from that truck as I could get.

I thought about just locking the doors, putting my head down, and going to sleep. I had this itch at the back of my neck though. Just a little something that said some undead madman with a machete and a hockey mask might be lingering nearby, waiting for me to sleep.

So just to be safe I pulled my tire thumper — like a mini baseball bat with a lead core — out from under the bench seat, yawned again, and got out to stretch my exhausted legs. I left my cell phone charging in the truck though. Didn't think I'd need it.

Felt weird to walk after so many hours on the road. Like maybe my balance was a little off. Or maybe the asphalt was a little off. Something like that. Made me bounce my steps a little more, twist my trunk, and wave my arms around. Try to work a little more juice through the old system.

Exercise had to be good for me, right? Get the blood moving, smell the fresh air, work the muscles. Get me ready to sleep. Except the air wasn't so fresh. Smelled like a surfeit of dead skunks. Almost enough to get me back behind the wheel and driving again.

Worse, the itch at the back of my neck wouldn't go away and kept me looking over my shoulder. Like some killer was just a few inches from spraying my brains all over the rest area. Didn't see anything though. Not yet.

I did find a coffee machine against one wall of the restroom building. The glass was cracked, but it didn't matter because the machine didn't work anyway. Ate four of my quarters proving its refusal to give me a single cup of regular, black.

What the rest stop did have an abundance of was huge red cedar trees surrounding it. That was where my nose led me. I needed some relief from the overpowering skunk smell and I figured that ten or fifteen minutes among the cedars might give me some light, pleasant peace.

Two dozen steps among the trees and I already felt better. This was my kind of place. This was where I belonged. With dirt, and grass, and moss, and leaves underfoot, rustling and crunching with each step. Where the night sky with its quarter-moon and its thousands of stars was a thing I could only barely see through the canopy—

Wait. The stars. The stars were wrong.

In Juneau we have light pollution, but not like down south of Canada. Every time I left town even a few miles, I could see more stars than I could count. Bright, big, beautiful stars. White stars, red stars, blue stars ... but not green stars. Not in a circle up in the sky where I expected to see Andromeda.

That itch at the back of my neck got sharp, and my stomach puckered in. I whipped around and saw a flicker of movement between two of the trees. I raised the tire thumper, my grip white-knuckled with fear.

"Come out!" I yelled. "I can see you there. I don't want trouble, but I'll use this thing if I have to."

More itching at the back of my neck and I spun around, tire thumper high and ready to swing...

But oh, God, he was beautiful. My height, with smooth skin as pale as the full moon and gorgeous lavender contact lenses. Long hair the color of a lion's mane, and features so fine he could have been crafted out of porcelain, from the sharp point of his chin to the sharp point of his ears.

And his clothes! Those boots had to have been doeskin, and they went all the way up to his knees. His shirt and pants like tailored honey, with little bits of amber for his buttons.

"How did you know I was here?" His voice could have been cracked out of the same cask of honey that his tailor worked from.

"Just ... I don't know. Paranoid." I felt like an awkward teen making conversation with my big crush. At least I managed not to fidget. "Ever since I parked. Like I'm being watched."

He tilted his head as he looked at me, and I swear I blushed like I was twelve again and not twice that age.

"What is your name?" he said.

"Lex. What's yours?"

He waited for a long moment, then said, "Son of..."

"My dad was Lars Frisk."

"Of course." He said something else. Something I couldn't quite hear. Sounded like viper or fighter. But I didn't care because he smiled then. Just a little raising of the corners of this mouth, but it was still fascinating. Suddenly I wasn't tired anymore. "Perhaps you should come have something to eat. If you will lower your club."

I still had the tire thumper up! Like I was going to strike him. As if I would. As if I *could*. I lowered my arm, and said the most eloquent thing I could think of.

"Lead on."

HE LED ME ALONG A PATH I HADN'T NOTICED BEFORE. SMOOTH DIRT. Like falling leaves never touched it. Just the light of the ... full moon? Sure enough. Full moon.

No itchy neck now. No smell of dead skunks either. Just a smell like cinnamon and the rich sound of laughter ahead and him, walking beside me. I felt like a stumbling buffoon. All elbows and ankles next to his grace. But it didn't seem to bother him. He looked over every so often, and he smiled when he did.

Finally we reached a clearing, with a huge roaring fire roasting what looked like an entire wild boar in the center and around it a circle of logs, each one at least a yard across.

And the people on those logs! A study in pale perfection. There had to have been twenty of them, all moving and talking and drinking and eating. They could have all been my escort's brothers and sisters. Not to say they all had his multicolored blonde locks. Some had hair as dark as a black bear, and others as red as a fox. But they all had his exquisite features, and eyes so bright and vivid they had to be contact lenses.

And they were all slender, though the women had curves aplenty. Their clothes were like their hair — all simple, tailored perfection, but varied in colors I might find on a day's hike in the forest.

One exception did stand out, and not just because of the high melanin count in his skin. On the other side of the fire from me sat this huge man. Like offensive lineman huge. He was wearing loose, patch-worn jeans, a Dallas Cowboys tee shirt under an open red flannel that matched mine, and a baseball hat advertising a common brand of American beer that even Jace wouldn't touch.

Didn't seem to bother our hosts, though. He was holding court to four girls who seemed just as utterly fascinated by him as I was by...

I still didn't know my escort's name.

I lost that thought when the big guy's eyes met mine, and we shared a moment of little kid glee. Like groupies who lucked into backstage passes to see our dream band. We didn't know how we got there, and we were trying to have fun while still terrified we'd get bounced.

He raised his frothy mug to me and my stomach rumbled so loud I wanted to curl up in a ball and die. That roasting boar smelled like heaven.

"You must be hungry," said my escort. He took me by the elbow and guided me to a spot on a log between him and his brunette twin, who handed me a plate full of boar meat and sliced apples.

Suddenly food was the only thing in the world. I devoured every bite on the plate with an intensity that ignored everyone else around me past the point of rudeness. But it was all so good. And I was so very hungry.

The boar meat was coming apart on my tongue, and so juicy I didn't even need the mug of cinnamon mead I found in my hand halfway through the meal. Not that I didn't drink it too. Then there were the apples. Crisp and sweet and juicy through every bite. Even the skins popped as I bit through them.

When I finished my second — or was it my third? — plate of food, I finally managed to look up at my escort's smile. I became very aware that he was sitting just close enough to be flirty. And so was his brunette twin, on my other side. Combine that with that huge fire and the food and mead in my belly and I was feeling very good.

And very awake. Should I have felt that awake?

I scratched at the back of my neck and the feeling went away.

"So, this is what you guys do?" I said. "Live in the woods and throw wild boar parties?"

"We are travelers," said the brunette, his voice a skosh deeper than my escort's. "We won't spend more than ... a night in this place."

"We never stay anywhere long," said my escort.

"Sounds lonely," I said, and kicked myself the moment I said it. But then, I wanted to kick myself after everything I'd said so far that evening. Every word out of my mouth sounded stupid and inadequate beside these people.

"Never," said my escort. "We have each other. And we make ... friends everywhere we go."

"I'll bet you do." I had to scratch my neck again. Something about the big guy holding court. I pointed to the man in question. "How long have you known him?"

"He arrived only hours before you did," said the brunette.

The big guy saw me pointing. "Hey! My name's Darrell!"

"Lex," I called back, and the manners my mother instilled in me from childhood itched at my neck. I stood up despite the hands of my escort and his brother, gentle on my shoulders to encourage me to stay.

Lots of surprised looks as I crossed to stand just between Darrell's harem and the fire. But my mother did not raise me to yell across the room, even when I was outside.

"Have a seat, buddy," said Darrell. "If the girls don't want to make room, maybe one will sit on your lap."

"I prefer their brothers," I said. "But how are you enjoying the party?"

"He's a party animal," said a redhead, rubbing Darrell's massive chest. "But our brothers are waiting for you."

"Better go," said Darrell with a smile so bright it rivaled the ... full moon above.

That thought made my neck itch a little as I turned away. But I felt like a colony of ants stampeded across my nape at the next thing Darrell said.

"Not good to keep a couple of Nubian princes waiting."

THE FIRE WASN'T GONE, BUT IT WAS COLD AND TINY COMPARED TO THE roar of even a moment before. And there was nothing roasting above it. Not even a squirrel.

But the moon above was still full, and there was still a circle of green stars high in the night sky. My stomach rumbled as it tried to sink. Fear, and the return of my hunger as though I hadn't eaten ... anything.

Worse, I was sick with exhaustion. My eyelids drooping. My mouth yawning so hard I felt my shoulders stretch, even though my neck was still itching like it would need a cheese grater to sate it. Seemed to take forever to turn my head and see Darrell sitting on a thin, rotted log and holding a leaf that dipped in the middle like a cup.

And Darrell was indeed surrounded by four women. Still pale, still wearing nice clothes but ... lesser somehow. Like they weren't goddesses anymore. Not even supermodels. Just human. Still maybe model hot, but definitely model skinny. Not the curvy temptresses they'd been a moment ago.

And all watching me, curiously, with those vibrant eyes. Such shocking colors that I almost missed their pointed ears. One of them narrowed her fuchsia eyes and I forced a quick lie of a smile. But what could I do? Their "brothers" were expecting me, but I was afraid of what I'd see when I turned and saw them.

"You all right, man?" said Darrell. "You look all ... ghostly."

"Yes," said the one with the fuchsia eyes. "I'd say you aren't altogether with us."

"Really?" I tried to sound casual over the heavy metal drumbeat of my heart. Terror was just about the only thing keeping my eyes open. "I was just realizing that had to be your semi parked out at the rest stop. Right Darrell?"

"Sure," he said, but his eyes were all about the girls.

Girls who looked him over like a piece of meat, which made me think uncomfortably about the "wild boar" that should have been roasting over that fire.

"Where did you find someone to give it that retro Nineties teal paint? It looks almost as old as I am."

"What?" said Darrell, blinking through the first syllable to come out of his mouth that didn't sound utterly thrilled to be here. "What do you mean? I just got it—"

One of the girls leaned in and kissed him, and Darrell's eyes closed in pleasure. I started hyperventilating. My knees shook with exhaustion. But my nape gave a sudden itch so sharp my head craned back before I could stop it.

Then I felt a hand on my shoulder. Without even looking I knew it was my escort.

I whipped around, wondering what happened to my tire thumper. Did I drop it back in the forest somewhere?

My escort faced me, his hands raised as though he meant no harm.

"Who are you people?" My voice came out a harsh whisper. "What are you?"

"Your grandfather would have called us *ljósálfar*."

"Elves?" Unspent adrenaline shook me. Made me even more tired. I was rocking on my feet.

"Something like that."

"You're not going to eat me!" Why couldn't I raise my voice to a shout like I wanted? "And I won't let you eat Darrell!"

"Eat you?" My escort laughed, and the sound was a tin echo of the mellifluous beauty the sound had been earlier. "We don't eat humans. In fact, your people are very important to our survival."

"Very..." I managed to turn my head at the speed of pouring molasses and saw Darrell's four girls leading him off into the shadows. Darrell gave me a thumb's up. I turned back blinking. I was too exhausted to make sense of this whole arrangement. I mean, if my escort was telling the truth, *Darrell* made sense. Just the kind of guy they needed. "But I ... and you...."

"Let me wake you up a little," said my escort, holding his right hand forward as though to touch me. "Otherwise you're going to fall over."

To his credit, he almost looked concerned. I nodded.

My escort touched me between the eyes with his middle finger, and muttered a few words that did sound kind of like Old Norse. Moments later I felt like the sun was rising all through my body and mind. Fresh dawn, fully rested. Strong and awake again.

Though that did mean I now remembered definitely dropping my tire thumper back in the woods a ways. Darn.

And my escort looked a little more beautiful and perfect than he had a moment before. But not so much as earlier, which the itch at the back of my neck said was a good thing, even if the rest of me was a little disappointed.

"Better?" he said.

"Kind of." I still wasn't sure how far I could trust it. "I get what you want with Darrell then, but what about me? I mean, yeah your sisters are beautiful and all, but that doesn't mean—"

"Of course not. But you are young, and healthy, and my brothers and I could entertain you for some time. And there would never have been a reason to draw your attention to what became of your seed."

Even wide awake I blinked in confusion at that one. Did he mean they switched genders? Or they had some magic way to...

No. I didn't want to know.

"So what are you going to do to me now?"

"That depends on you. You are between right now. Not really with us, but not really home either. You must have a touch of *seiðr* about you, though you haven't trained it at all. If you like, I could bring you back to the party and show you a very good time. We would love to blend your magic with ours as we did of old."

Seiðr? Like a seer? Interesting idea, but I had a more immediately important point to worry about.

"What do you mean party? That was all illusion."

My escort laughed, and I had to admit that his laugh was sounding better. And he had a flirty look to those lavender eyes.

"Come with me to the party and I will explain it all." He bit his lip. "But we will not force you. If you prefer, I will take you the rest of the way back to your world."

I admit, I was tempted. A night of no-strings fun sounded like just what the doctor ordered for a broken heart...

Except that it wasn't really no-strings fun. I would be fathering little elf children. Maybe just one. Maybe a whole bunch. I had no way of knowing. I knew I wanted kids one day, but not like that. Of course, I'd probably never meet them, or even knew that they'd been born. And since they'd be living here with—

That was when my escort's last two words hit me. *My world*? This was another *world*? My terror at all the illusions came screaming back by way of my nape. My next words all but flew out of my mouth.

"Yes! Take me back!"

MY ESCORT SAID NOTHING AS WE WALKED BACK DOWN THE CLEAR PATH together. Then the path faded and I was once more among the sights and smells of the grove of red cedars that surrounded that old, beat-up rest stop.

I turned to say goodbye, but my escort was gone.

That was when I realized it was broad daylight. But I still wasn't tired. Warm, too. Very warm for this time of year. Had to be flirting with sixty or sixty five degrees. Freak pressure system, I guessed.

I shook my head. Elves. My mom would never believe it all. Much less Jace. Made me hope he'd been trying to call my cell phone, which was still charging back in the truck. I then hated myself for the thought. The hell with Jace.

Hot elf boys wanted a piece of me. I wasn't going back to a cheater.

I made my way back through the trees, glancing every step to see if I could spot my tire thumper, but I couldn't see a sign of it. Lost forever, I imagine.

I was about ten steps from the edge of the tree line when I realized that the time of day wasn't the only thing that had changed. There were flowers blooming here among the cedars. Three kinds of wildflowers I could spot without craning my neck. I blew out my air and inhaled through my nose as deeply as my lungs allowed.

Spring. I smelled spring. Fresh growth. Blooming wildflowers.

Whoa.

A wave of cold that had nothing to do with the playful little breeze ran all the way down my spine and nestled in my boots. Just how long had that party—

Then I remembered Darrell's truck, with its teal paint job that screamed Nineties at me. But he hadn't looked older than maybe thirty...

Mom.

I ran back to the rest stop as fast as I could. The skunk smell was gone. The itch at the back of my neck was gone. Darrell's semi was gone.

My truck was gone.

I fell to my knees there in the parking lot and screamed. Hot tears streamed down my face. Gone. My life was gone. My mother—

"You must be the one," said a woman's high, soft voice.

I heard the words, but I barely noticed them. Everything I knew. Every*one* I knew. Oh, God.

I felt a hand on my shoulder. Comforting. That was what finally got me to turn my head. Young redheaded woman with eyes like emeralds. Tall and slender, in tight jeans and an equally tight tee-shirt for some band I didn't know.

But then, all the bands I knew were probably gone too.

Tears kept flowing, and I didn't try to stop them. Or my snuffling. But I did manage to say, "Huh?"

"I said you must be the one. The one who went to party with the *sidhe*. My mom said you'd be coming back today, and asked me to come talk to you."

None of this made sense. And I wasn't the type of guy to want to party with any *she* anyway. But at that moment I kept crying about my mom — who was dead for all I knew — and my life.

"Mom ended up at a party like that once, but she keeps to the old ways. The moment she got back she tried to set things up here so no one would want to stop ever again. Much less go wander into the woods. She figures you must have a touch of the second sight." The redhead shrugged. "Anyway, the cards told her a man would—"

"Do you have a phone?"

"Oh, Brigid! I'm sorry." She slapped herself in the forehead and pulled a small device out of her front pocket. "Of course. Call anyone you want."

She had to show me how to use it, but soon enough my mom's number was ringing.

Three rings.

Four.

Five.

Connection. That alone made me sigh, until I heard the voice on the other end. A young woman with a noncommittal hello.

"May I please speak to Ingrid Frisk?"

"Who may I say is calling?"

Relief hit me so hard I slumped onto the warm asphalt.

"This is her son Alexander."

"One moment."

That moment felt like centuries. While I waited the redhead moved off to a polite distance and made a show of looking away.

"Alex? Is it really you?"

Her voice sounded so frail I started blubbering. But somewhere in there I managed to get out the words, "It's ... me ... Mom."

She joined me crying. We bawled at each other for what felt like at least half an hour before either of us was coherent enough to form words.

"Alex, where have you been?"

"Mom, you're not going to believe this."

◊◊◊◊◊

FROZEN

FROZEN

There are moments in life when you wish time would stop, and moments when it actually does. The former are usually the best moments. Love and friendship and fun. But the latter, well, it only happened to me once.

Too late at night for the speed I was driving. Especially in the rain. But I was eighteen and convinced of my immortality, like we all were at that age. Considering I had to be up at six a.m. to open Dream On Records – the last actual record store in Santa Josita, California, just another Bay Area suburb – I had no business staying at that party until two. But I did.

What can I tell you? Trina Dalman was talking to me. *Me.* As in, the party was going on inside Pierre's parents' place, and it was just the Blonde Goddess Herself and *me* on the patio. Both of us finding excuses to keep the other talking until we made an honest-to-God date for Saturday night.

Yeah, it was a stupid date – mini-golf and pizza – but it was going to be just the two of us, and she'd already hinted that she loved the view from that rest area up Skyline Drive. And I knew what view *I* wanted to see on Skyline Drive.

So, yeah, maybe I'd been awake some twenty hours, but I was so bouncy excited about my date that I was sure I could have run all the way home if I had to. Even in the rain. Driving seemed like nothing.

I had Three Coyotes cranked up on the stereo of The Fossil, which was what I called my 1992 Pontiac Sunfire, and was blazing my way up 280N from San Jose. 280N was everything a freeway ought to be – wide and smooth, with lots of lanes, and rises and dips, and enough curves to keep me thinking of Trina. I still had the taste of light beer in my mouth, but I hadn't had a drop in over an hour to make sure I was safe to drive.

Usually, driving 280 at that hour meant that most of the lights I'd see were on the side of the freeway along the hills, so green in the wintertime. Most nights, the view in my rearview mirror would be black as outer space, and up ahead I'd be lucky to see one or two cars over the whole thirty-mile stretch from Pierre's parents' place.

Most nights. But not that night.

The freeway wasn't exactly *packed*, but it felt that way because I was in a hurry. Cars were scattered everywhere, and they all seemed to be doing that I'm-not-drunk thing. That thing where they'd weave just a little in their lanes, and drive about three miles off the actual speed limit, either a little high or a little low or varying between the two.

It was as though everyone was having their Christmas party two weeks early, all on the same rainy night, and the partygoers had dipped into the eggnog a little heavy before driving home.

And I did not have time for speed limit driving. So I just pretended the cars were asteroids and wove between and around them at high speed, laughing and whooping and still high-fiving myself about having a date with *Trina Dalman*.

I was just turning back to face front after leveling a Monty Python insult at some idiot. Honestly. Driving his red Lexus Coupe under the speed limit in the fast lane. He hit his horn at me. I hit mine at him. Some other people were hitting theirs, but I couldn't see who.

Then I got my eyes forward again, and I saw the worst sight this side of hell.

Brake lights. Everywhere.

All four lanes ahead of me were full, and they were all stopped. Some of them must have been adding to the horn symphony.

They'd been hidden by a curve and an incline, and my looking behind me hadn't helped. Exhausted and giddy as I was, even if I'd been going the speed limit on dry ground, I might have been hard-pressed to stop in time. As it was...

Crash. Incoming. Maybe three seconds.

Three.

I slammed on the brakes. They locked. My tires screamed for mercy on the wet pavement.

Two.

I tried whipping the wheel away. Tried to aim for the guardrail. Steering wheel locked. I was bound straight for the rear bumper of a great big SUV, complete with Baby On Board bumper sticker, and tons of camping gear strapped to the roof.

One.

I yanked my emergency brake and closed my eyes.

I STOPPED?

That was my first thought when I opened my eyes. It didn't make sense, but I actually thought for a moment that I managed to halt my speeding car.

I actually got as far as whooping before pieces of the scene around me started clicking in my head, and they didn't add up to a coherent puzzle.

First, my car wasn't scant inches from the bumper of that SUV. I had to be a good twenty feet back, which was just about exactly how far back I'd been when I yanked the emergency brake.

Second, it was quiet. Like dead-of-night-in-a-closet-hiding-from-your-brother quiet. No more honking horns. No squeal of my brakes. No drumming of the rain. Even my music stopped.

Third, and that this was third and not first tells you something about my state of mind, I was just sitting comfortably in my seat. No deploying airbags trying to protect me from my sudden stop. No chest pain from getting thrown against the seat belt.

Those were all things that came and went through my mind in short order, dizzying in their nonsensicalness. What cemented for me that something was wrong was what I saw next.

The Lexus Coupe. In my rear view mirror.

Frozen.

I might not have been in the best state of mind, but I'd been guessing that the Lexus driver had been tippling from the eggnog a little more than most of my fellow drivers because I just couldn't imagine why else he would have been driving under the speed limit in the fast lane of a freeway built for speed at freaking two-fifteen in the morning.

Then I saw his face. Moments before, he'd been business-man arrogant, with his Clark Kent haircut and his judgmental eyebrows as he'd pounded the horn at me.

Now, his face was frozen in a scream.

Frozen.

That was when I realized the rain had stopped mid-downpour. And I don't mean the rain went away. I mean I could see hundreds of droplets hanging in the air, halted on their way to the ground.

That made all the pieces slam together in my head. Jingly cold jolted through my system. I screamed, and it came out louder than ever in all that silence.

I lost a minute or two, just manic. I beat on the horn – which didn't blare – I yanked on the emergency brake – which was already high as it would go. I saw that my speedometer still read fifty miles per hour and panic just ripped right through me.

I had to get out. I was going to crash and I had to get out.

I popped the seat belt, threw open my door and dove onto the asphalt.

I rolled to a halt against stiff green grass, that didn't particularly want to yield just because I was bumping up against it. I felt the bumps, but none of it hurt. I expected at least a scuffed elbow or a bruised thigh, but when I stopped rolling, I felt fine. A little wet from diving through raindrops and rolling on wet ground, but otherwise normal.

I got up. Patted myself off as I looked around. No one else was moving. Everyone else seemed to be frozen in that single instance. I could see two little toe-headed kids in the SUV looking back at my car as though it never occurred to them that it might hit them.

The idiot in the Lexus still staring straight forward, mid-scream. No sign that he'd seen me dive out of my car.

My car door was still open though. That was something. Some small sign of change in this weird fever dream.

What was the last thing I did? The last thing before everything froze?

I yanked on my e-brake. And I prayed. Did I pray? I assume I must have. No atheists in foxholes and all that jazz.

Was that what this was? Was some god, some guardian angel maybe, stopping the world in answer to my prayer?

"Hello?" I called. "Anybody?"

I tried to remember the name of that angel from *It's a Wonderful Life*, but it just wouldn't come. Couldn't have been the same angel anyway. That guy got his wings at the end of the movie.

Didn't matter. Nobody answered me anyway, even though I called a few more times.

By now the shock was wearing off and curiosity set in. Just what was happening and why? Maybe I'd had an accident, and I was in a coma. Making this some sort of coma fantasy. Or maybe a half-conscious fugue state where I was trying to piece my life back together, but when I woke up I'd have amnesia or something.

Seemed pretty coherent for a fugue state though. Detailed too. No two of the raindrops were quite identical. And I could get up close and personal to look. They were slightly different lengths and thicknesses.

I ... I don't know why I lost time trying to find a pattern in the raindrops. I think maybe I'd convinced myself that there was some kind of secret hidden among them. That whatever was going on was, in fact, a divine act. Even if no choirs of angels showed up to sing answers to me in three-part harmony.

No way to know how much time I wasted that way. Wasn't as though the clock on my phone was changing. It was stuck at two-fifteen and fifty-eight seconds.

The other reason it was hard to gauge how long I wasted that way, was that I wasn't changing either. I mean, my heart wasn't pounding the way it was when I grabbed the e-brake, but I still had that jittery adrenaline I'm-going-to-die sense all through my body. Still had that cold fear too, even if it didn't really demand my attention anymore.

All right. I've got to be honest with you, even though this is the freakiest part for me to even think about.

I'm pretty sure my heart wasn't beating.

I was moving around, and I must have been breathing because I sure had enough air to let me scream and yell. But when I realized I still felt that adrenaline rush, I tried to take my pulse.

Nothing.

Not at either wrist. Not at my neck. I even pressed my fingertips to my chest in three places, trying to find a heartbeat. And I found nothing.

That was enough to send another jolt of fear through me, but the adrenaline and jitters didn't get any worse.

I knew it then. I had to be dead.

Deciding I was dead actually sent a wave of peace through me. Didn't stop the jitters or the bounciness, even if I felt a little sad that I wouldn't live to go on that date with Trina. But still, dead, right? As in, all my cares were gone now and I got to find out what happened next.

Except that if this was next, nothing was happening.

"So," I called out to the rain-cloud-filled heavens above. "What happens now? Does the grim reaper come to collect me? An angel, maybe? A Valkyrie?

"Is anyone even listening?"

No answer.

Well, I was not going to stand here not getting any older while some cosmic bureaucratic snafu kept me in limbo.

I started checking out the other cars. I figured maybe, just maybe, there was someone else dead like me, and sitting in their car. Maybe just as puzzled as I was. Or maybe even more puzzled, if they hadn't figured out the dead part yet.

I made sure not to look back at my car as I started into the crowd of traffic ahead of me. One, I figured my dead body might be sitting behind the wheel, and who needed to see that? And two, if the car door was open, then that might indicate I was still corporeal, and thus not actually dead. And I was starting to groove a bit on the notion of being dead, so if I was wrong, I didn't want to harsh my buzz just yet.

Typical Bay Area mix of cars, by which I mean everything from old heaps held together by rust and prayers all the way up to six-figure beasts by Ferrari and Tesla, with the ages and nationalities of their passengers as diverse as the makes and models of cars.

The only consistent thing? They were all frozen.

I must have checked some fifty cars on my way to the front of this mess, and in every single one, every single passenger was frozen. Even the babies and animals, 'cause I wasn't discounting any possibilities here.

But nope. I was the only one up and about, all the way up to the front of the line. Up at the front, a few of the drivers were getting out of their cars, but they were frozen mid-attempt.

Two car wreck causing all this traffic, blocking four lanes. One of the cars was an old tank of a station wagon that someone had managed to keep running since the 1970s. The other was a late model SUV, the kind with all the bells and whistles.

The right front bumper on the station wagon was ripped clean off. The rear left bumper of the SUV was wrecked hard enough to snap the axle, if the angle of the wheel was any indication.

The station wagon had the kind of family my dad would call trailer park trash, whether or not they lived in a trailer park. Pasty white and overweight, all six of them. But they'd all had their seat-belts on and looked no worse for wear.

The SUV had a Japanese American family, five of them. They looked fine too. Airbags all deployed. Didn't see any blood or pained expressions. Panicked and worried expressions aplenty, but nobody who looked hurt.

The dads of both families had been driving, but they were out of their cars and looked to have been frozen mid-yelling match in the middle of the freeway.

Farther down the freeway I could see two highway patrol cars coming, driving the wrong way down the empty section of freeway. Well, they'd been driving when time stopped, anyway. In that instant, they might as well have been ten miles away.

Everything looked under control. Bad, sure, but nothing fatal. Nothing that seemed to me to be worth stopping time on this end.

That was when I saw the doll.

It was a little Wonder Woman doll, sitting in the middle of the fast lane, maybe two dozen feet from the SUV. My eyes tracked from the doll to the SUV, where a little girl in the backseat was staring out the half-open car window at the doll.

She already had one hand going for the door latch.

I looked back up the freeway at the inbound patrol cars. The drivers' eyes were fixed on the mid-freeway confrontation.

They might not even see one little girl toddling onto the asphalt for a doll.

And what about the front line of the impatient cars behind me? What if one of those drivers tried to go around?

Seemed like the most obvious thing in the world for me to pick up the doll and put it in the hand of the little girl reaching for the door latch.

I have to admit. When I did, I half-expected that this was the magic key. That I was here, in a moment of frozen rainstorm on a freeway, to save a little girl's life. That maybe, when I put the doll back in her hand, I'd find myself back behind the wheel of The Fossil that magically managed to avoid an accident because I'd done the Right Thing (trademark pending).

That wasn't how it worked.

WHEN I FINISHED RANTING MY DISAPPOINTMENT AT MY CONTINUED imprisonment between seconds, I wandered back toward my car.

I confess. I did consider just walking away somewhere. Home, maybe, or back to see Trina even if she couldn't see me. And I'd like to say that the reason I didn't was that it would have felt ghostly, that I would have felt alone and cut off from the world. All that teenage angst crap.

Honestly, though, it just felt too darn far to walk. Maybe I wouldn't get any more tired than I already was, but I really didn't have any way to know that. I just knew when I thought about the distances involved, all I really wanted to do was go back to my car and await the inevitable. Whatever it turned out to be.

Personally, I was hoping the inevitable brought a breakfast burrito.

But when I got back to my car – door open and no dead me inside – I didn't climb back inside.

Instead, I looked at the angle. I mean, the car was still going about fifty, though the emergency brake would have something to say about that, and my efforts at spinning the steering wheel hadn't done enough to clear the bumper of that huge, camping-gear-laden SUV. An SUV with two families inside and about ten people altogether.

From the way I judged the angle, my car was bound to hit that bumper. Maybe to the left side instead of dead on, but I was still pretty sure "dead" would end up being the key word before all the smoke cleared.

So I climbed up on top of the SUV and started looking through the camping gear. Handing the doll to the little girl had made me think – no matter what happened to me, time had to start again eventually, and there had to be some way to get my car to miss that SUV.

I found a good, solid wooden oar. I jammed that oar under the front right tire of my car just as hard as I could. Didn't get far, but it would be enough for some traction.

I had to hunt among the hills at the side of the road to find a big enough rock to do the job I had in mind. It also had to be one I could carry, but past a certain point, size was only going to do so much good anyway.

I got the rock under the oar at what I hoped was the right spot.

That was when time started again.

THE REST SHOWED UP IN THE ACCIDENT REPORT. MY CAR WAS SPEEDING right for that rock, when the oar fell in my path. Wedged my car on two wheels, where it flipped onto the shoulder. Missed the SUV by maybe six inches.

Luckiest guy in the world that I was that day, I got thrown clear before The Fossil rolled. Paramedics found me on the side of the road, half-conscious but generally unharmed. Mostly in shock, they said.

The Fossil was totaled, but I was still able to keep my date with Trina the next night. And I had one heck of a story to tell her.

IF YOU KILL HITLER....

IF YOU KILL HITLER....

Willie didn't figure time travel would change anything.

Sure, he heard about the discovery on the news, same as everyone else. Thing was, he figured it didn't apply to him. Discovery that big, no doubt the government was going to conscript and redact and twist and pontificate, until the only people who ever got to make use of the discovery were the sort who signed their lives away to government service.

Willie wasn't a big believer in government "service." Not since he got out. Volunteering, that was service he could get behind. Food kitchens every Saturday. Playing guitar for people on hospice every Tuesday and Thursday afternoon. That was service. That was making a difference in people's lives.

The government stuff, he'd seen enough of in his two-year stint as a grunt. Living under threat in bad conditions to shoot bullets at people over ... some political disagreement or other.

Six countries in twenty-four months. Must have fired off more rounds than he earned dollars during that time. And it was during those two years that Willie did something that, well, no amount of volunteer service could ever make up for.

So, yeah, maybe time travel didn't apply to guys like Willie.

Still.

When he heard about time travel on the noisy television up over
the counter at the Gravy Caboose – his personal favorite greasy spoon
because of how well they made chicken waffles with gravy fries – he
had a fleeting thought that maybe, just maybe, he could go back in
time himself.

Be Private Willie McTavish one more time, to set right what he
did that day...

THE JUNGLE MAY NOT HAVE BEEN HOTTER THAN THE DESERT WAS, BUT
here the heat clung as bad as the stinky mud. Heat so damp it was like
Willie woke up sweating. Like his shorts never made it into the dryer,
but he had to wear them anyway, and his fatigues were even worse.

And "fatigues" was right. Damp as they were, they must have
weighed ten pounds more than normal. Not something he noticed
first thing in the morning, but after that afternoon march, then the
firefight with the "rebels" – harsh term for people fighting for their
own way of life, which Willie considered none of his business – just
wearing them was exhausting. His clothes felt like lead and his pack
so heavy he might have been carrying his whole platoon.

Maybe not the *whole* platoon. Maybe just the ones who'd died in
the firefight. Hicks, Brayburn, Collins, and Devereaux.

Only eight guys in Willie's squad still among the living when they
found that burned out village. And it was a village, not a town or a
city. Willie's squad been briefed on this. There were still small tribes
in Africa. Nomads mostly. Not part of any one nation, but allowed to
go their own way as long as they stuck to certain restricted areas,
because the muckety-mucks had decreed it. And because Uncle Sam
gave the affected nations money.

There were reasons. Willie didn't care.

All he cared about right then was a place to drop for a little while.
Close his eyes. Let his heart rate get back to something like normal.

Maybe get the chance to unclench his shoulders and jaw. Take a minute to think about the dead. Maybe say a prayer.

The village wasn't much. Grass and wicker huts over a dry dirt clearing. Mostly burned away, but a few walls left to give something like shelter. More important was the dry dirt. "Dry" was like a half-remembered dream.

The sergeant didn't want to stop. Said the villages were keep-away zones for us G.I. Joes. The ell tee overruled him. Said it was burnt out by the locals to drive the tribe away before the fighting came close. Said other things too, but by the time he got to them, the rest of the squad was horizontal and it didn't much matter.

Mattered to Sarge.

Willie'd been the first one to drop his pack on the lovely dry ground, so Willie was the first of two named to perimeter guard. Not enough of the squad left for a proper perimeter, and they all needed rest something fearsome, so Willie got one one-eighty and Johnson got the other.

Getting back up was Hell. Holding his rifle again was worse. But worst of all, he had the one-eighty facing the jungle. Ferns and trees and flowers in wild colors. That damp, decay smell like it was all dying right in front of him, the way Devereaux had.

Every inch of it could have hidden guys who wanted nothing more than to shoot Willie. Or at least who were willing to pull the trigger at Willie for traveling thousands of miles and trying to tell them they were on the wrong side.

Willie's arms were shaking, holding the rifle. His eyes teared up. So very tired, but his heart was pounding like it was trying to outrun stampeding elephants. Every crack and snap jerked his head, every strange bird cry raised his rifle.

Willie was going to die here. He was sure of it.

Then it happened. A face popped into view. And there was a rifle. Willie was sure he saw a rifle. Absolutely positive in the moment that just under that ink-dark face, a rifle came up like it was going to point at him in the next second or two.

Willie stopped breathing. Couldn't hear anything but the rush of his own blood.

This was it. Him or this "rebel." This poor soul who had nothing against Willie except that Willie was where he was, doing what he was doing. This poor bastard who had more right to shoot Willie than Willie had to shoot him.

But the instinct to survive was a powerful, powerful thing.

Willie only had maybe a second. But in that time his rifle sprang into firing position.

A burst of automatic weapon fire made the air stink of gunpowder. Made the rifle even hotter in Willie's blistered and clenching hands.

Maybe the same moment. Maybe just after. Willie wasn't sure, exactly. But the rest of the squad, they started shooting too.

Tore up that little patch of jungle something fierce.

Turned out, wasn't rebels, and they weren't armed. Villagers, where they weren't supposed to be. Hiding from the war, instead of moving on to someplace safe.

No cameras and no witnesses. Didn't matter. Willie confessed the whole thing right to the colonel when they got back to the base. Spent days waiting for the M.P.s. The tribunal.

Wasn't 'til later he found out, the ell tee and the colonel were old family friends. That the colonel buried the incident – and Willie's report – the way the squad buried the bodies.

Deep.

JUST ABOUT NINETY DAYS AFTER THE WORST DAY IN WILLIE'S LIFE, HE was discharged. Word was, the whole squad was, minus the ell tee, and Sarge. Honorable, according to the forms.

After Willie'd filled out those forms, two guys in black suits had come in and made very, very clear to Willie that he was never to talk about that day, or he'd spend the rest of his life in a rubber room.

Just about three years after the worst day in Willie's life, he still woke up sweating. Still wondered what the hell he'd thought was a rifle. Branch, maybe?

And it was that incident that Willie thought of as he sat at the counter of the Gravy Caboose and watching the news segment about time travel.

Willie daydreamed about going back in time. Stopping himself from shooting, maybe. Or maybe just getting those villagers to flee to safety. He liked the latter idea better. Figured it had a better chance of making sure those poor villagers stayed safe.

Didn't matter though, and Willie knew it. Time travel, that was for the muckety-mucks. Or maybe for the rich, and Willie was a lot of things, but rich wasn't one of them.

So Willie tried not to get his hopes up. Tried to ignore the follow-up stories and in-depth articles and exposés and all the other segments about time travel over the coming months.

Wasn't easy. Even the sports section talked about how time travel might affect records we've always thought of as set in stone. DiMaggio's hitting streak. Cy Young's wins. Settle questions like who knew what about the Black Sox scandal, and whether or not Rose gambled on the sport.

Just when things reached the point that Willie was ready to give up on the news altogether, the time travel stories just stopped. Maybe they actually faded away like most news stories do, but to Willie it seemed as though one day the stories were freaking everywhere, and the next the news was back to murders and politics. Business as usual.

Guy, at the counter of the Gravy Caboose, tried to make some kind of conspiracy theory about it. Got his voice all hush-hush and went on about how the government had the real thing and they were keeping it quiet and such like.

Willie didn't see the point of the hush-hush tones. Figured it never could have been any other way. If there was time travel, of course the government controlled it.

And Willie continued to think that. Right up to the grand opening of Time of Your Life, the first time travel center in the Bay Area.

Mountain View, to be exact. Dead center of Silicon Valley, of course, which made it not much more than twenty miles from Willie's apartment down in Gilroy.

Willie tried to ignore it. Wasn't easy, because the news did "features" and spot segments, not to mention the place did a metric ton of advertising. But Willie figured it was for the rich people. The Silicon Valley billionaires, or the venture capitalists, or just the old money Atherton types.

But then the dream came back.

Every night, Willie was back in that village. Every night he was pulling the trigger. But it wasn't just the covering jungle he saw getting blown apart. Wasn't just the smell of gunpowder and the chatter of his rifle. No. In the dream, he saw every face. Heard every scream. Smelled their blood and their perforated bowels.

And every time, Willie woke up screaming and sweating.

Willie survived three months of that before he couldn't take it anymore. If it took every dollar he had, if it took the rest of his life to pay it off, Willie had to go back. He had to make things right.

He had to.

The Time of Your Life parking lot wasn't small — the place looked like a converted grocery store, complete with plenty of parking – but it was *jammed*. Willie rumbled around for about ten minutes in his beat-up old Chevy S-10 pickup before he gave up and found street parking about two blocks away.

Willie'd been hoping that a Saturday morning in the spring would have been empty at a place like that. Hoped his breakfast shift at the shelter let him out early enough to beat the crowds.

Apparently he was wrong.

The inside of the place was done in blue and purple swirls of tile, and it had colorful posters of different times and places. Victorian parties. Gladiator fights in ancient Rome. The deck of the Titanic. The battle of Bannockburn. Woodstock and about a dozen other concert posters. The coronations of Queen Elizabeth II, Henry V, and others. More posters and times than Willie could begin to count.

One prominent poster, bigger than the others, showed a black and white photo of Hitler in his Nazi uniform, with huge yellow letters that read: "Kill Hitler!"

Willie did wonder how much they could charge for that, given that it could only be done once.

The cross-section of people all sitting around the huge lobby and filling out forms was amazing. Young and old, some in the latest fashions, others with clothes almost falling apart. Seemed that not only did everyone *want* to travel through time, but maybe, just maybe, everyone could *afford* it. Maybe not the Hitler package, but the chance to fix some misstep in life, to right some small wrong.

Or maybe, like Willie, some of them had a really, really big wrong to set right.

The harried lady at the counter shoved a clipboard with a form at Willie, gave him a number tag – Willie's number was three eighty-six – and turned away to the next customer.

Willie found a seat off near the front window, next to a ficus, at the end of a row that held one big family. They all had pleasant features, well-groomed hair and clothes, and spoke in excited, hushed tones about meeting someone named Smith.

The form didn't take Willie long. Mostly health questions and disclaimers. Willie'd filled out hundreds of forms like that in the service. Sure, on this one he had to lie in a couple of places, but that was par for the course. Truth was, Willie didn't care if he came back broken, crazy or dead. Not so long as he saved those villagers.

Waiting for his number, that took a little longer. But waiting was another skill honed to a fine edge in the service. Rush, rush, rush, then sit on your hands for hours on end before it's rush, rush, rush again.

Willie didn't miss that.

Finally, though, Willie's number was called.

IT WASN'T AN OFFICE, SO MUCH AS A CUBICLE AMONG A GOOD DOZEN. That same gray cloth for the walls that Willie saw every time a delivery took him past the front desk of one company or another. This one smelled like aerosol potpourri.

In the cubicle, just a man with a keyboard, sitting in a leather executive chair. He wore a black suit – jacket draped over the back of the chair – but a vivid purple tie over his crisp, white shirt. His haircut was just as crisp. Sarge would've approved. He wore big glasses, the kind that had a computer HUD where he could see it and Willie couldn't.

"Sit down, sit down," the man said with a smile full of bright teeth. He kept talking before Willie could even sit in the red, rolling visitor's chair. "You look like the ex-military type. Let me guess."

He looked Willie up and down. Pointed his finger at him. "You want to kill Hitler?"

"No, I, uh—"

"Because if you kill Hitler, be sure to get the tee shirt on this visit. We don't keep records of where you went or what you did, so after you leave there'll be no way to prove you qualify for the shirt."

"I'm not here for Hitler."

"Oh. Want to try your luck with Marilyn Monroe? We don't sell a tee shirt for this one, but—"

"No!" Willie was sweating now. His heart was pounding, and this guy wouldn't shut up.

"Hey," the man said, raising his hands in surrender, "we're not talking rape here. Our historians just happened to find out about this one party where the sex goddess herself showed up looking for Mr. Right Now, and—"

"*Let me talk!*"

"I'm sorry," the man said with that big smile. "It's just that the possibilities are so endless, we want to make sure you understand your options."

"I know exactly what I want to do."

Willie was sitting forward in the chair now, bouncing a little the way he used to, when he knew a fight was coming. Like his body was going to make sure it was ready, whether he wanted it to or not. And he had the same loose, watery feeling in his bowels, perfect contrast to a mouth so dry he had to clear his throat before he could talk.

It was while Willie was clearing his throat that the man actually lost that smile. Got a sympathetic expression on his face. He reached down somewhere behind him and grabbed a bottle of water. Spoke in gentle tones while Willie drank.

"This is a personal thing, isn't it? Either you want to go back for the one that got away, or you made some huge mistake that you want to fix. Right?"

"Mistake. Big one."

"Don't tell me any details," the man said quickly. "Especially if it involves breaking the law. We have to report anything like that."

"How can you send me—"

"If you've got something specific, something outside our usual packages, all we need are the date and location. What you do there is your business."

Willie nodded. Pulled out his notebook with the date and the GPS coordinates, as near as he could glean the latter from the internet. He started to hand them to the man, but the man put his hands up again.

"Let me give you some advice," the man said. He shook his head. "Don't do this."

"I need to," Willie said, putting every bit of whatever soul he had left into those words.

"All the more reason you shouldn't," the man said. "Look, haven't you—"

"*I have to make it right!*"

"Haven't you seen the news?"

Willie shook his head.

The man sighed. "Let me put it this way. Today alone, probably two hundred people are going to try to kill Hitler. Hell, a good half of them, at least, will succeed."

Willie was only half-listening. His lips were open now, and he knew he was panting. He was so close now. Why did this man delay him?

"Maybe half as many will try to nail Marilyn Monroe. Or Jane Mansfield. Or somebody like that. Or they'll try to save Jack Kennedy on that day in Texas, and a bunch of them will succeed too. Why do you think so many people can do those things?"

Willie just stared blankly at the man. There was some sense in those words, somewhere, but Willie couldn't puzzle it past his heartbeat.

"You can't change the past," the man said. "Time travel seems to work, but truth is it either creates one hell of a delusion, or it creates alternate timelines. The timeline version is more popular with scientists, but personally I like the delusion angle. It means we aren't messing up whole other worlds just for our own amusement."

Willie was stuck on one sentence there.

"You can't change the past?"

"Nope." The man shook his head firmly. "You could kill Hitler every day for a month, but World War II still happened, complete with death camps. You could seduce Monroe every day for a year, but she'd never leave that night pregnant, no matter how fertile you are. Hell, you could kill Lee Harvey Oswald all you like. He'll still shoot Jack Kennedy."

He leaned forward, his eyes boring right through Willie.

"Whatever you want to go back and change, you can't. You said what you said. You did what you did. My advice? Forget time travel and go see a therapist."

Willie started to get up, but stopped and dropped back down into his chair.

"Wait," Willie said. "You said something about alternate timelines?"

"It's just a theory."

Willie looked at the man until he sighed.

"You can't change *our* past. That's fixed. But some of the scientists, they think that if you go back and make a change, the time stream branches off. Creates a world where whatever you changed becomes *that world's* past."

The man must have seen the light come into Willie's eye, because he rushed to add, "Doesn't change anything here though. You get back to the exact same world you left. Whatever you really did is still what really happened."

"But if I" – Willie saw the man's hands waving him to shut up – "*hypothetically*, went back to a time and place where I could save a bunch of lives—"

"Those people would still be just as dead."

"Here. But in another world..."

The man sighed again. Sagged in his chair. Defeat in his voice as he said, "In another world, maybe – *maybe* – they'll still be alive. If that theory's true. You *may* just be fooling yourself."

Willie gave a helpless shrug.

"That's a chance I have to take."

NO SHORTCUTS TO FAME

NO SHORTCUTS TO FAME

I woke up staring at myself.

That alone should have been enough to have me screaming in terror, but I was still rumpled and half-asleep, and figured I was dreaming.

I mean, it was definitely my own double bed, and from the Halestorm and Ozzy posters on the walls, this was definitely my small bedroom. My small apartment in Sunnyvale, California. I could smell the remains of last night's midnight burrito, on my nightstand. See the half-empty glass of water next to its plate.

Besides, many of my dreams started with me waking up. Weird, but I figured it was a side effect of studying lucid dreaming.

So I rubbed sleep out of my eyes and yawned and looked up at the me who was standing over my bed, looking back at me. Hair tied back in a ponytail. That me had the worried expression I knew so well: bushy brown eyebrows furrowed, and lips pulled to the right side.

"Am I dreaming?" I asked, figuring I'd get an honest answer from myself.

"Have you been there yet?" the standing me said. He was wearing my Black Sabbath "The End" tour tee shirt, and my favorite faded blue jeans. And he hadn't shaved, which wasn't like me.

"Am. I. Dreaming?" I repeated, focused now. Trying to spot any little discrepancies that might constitute a dream sign. But the band name on the Halestorm poster stayed looking exactly the same, no matter how many times I flicked my eyes away and back. And the digital clock on my nightstand consistently insisted it was four a.m exactly.

Not a single dream sign.

Cold fear washed over me, followed by the lightest sheen of sweat.

The standing me shook his head, quickly.

"No," he said. "You're not dreaming, and I don't have time to explain. You need to head out to—"

And then he popped like a soap bubble.

I screamed.

Not loud and long like a horror movie. *That* would have been kind of cool. But no. My scream came out little more than the kind of yip a teenage girl might make.

I was the lead singer of a metal band that was just starting to pick up a real following. I had the kind of looks and stage presence that got girls to throw their panties and their phone numbers at me during a show. Got them to email me the kinds of photos they might not even show their boyfriends.

But when I was scared, all that cool went right out the window. Embarrassing, but true.

I jumped out of bed. Brushed back my hair, then grabbed a hair tie off the closet doorknob and bound back my chestnut brown sleep snarls. Paced naked back and forth.

I couldn't be awake. But I had to be awake.

I glanced over at the clock again. Four-oh-two a.m. now.

Damn it. I had to be awake.

Then I really saw that?

I stopped and stared at the spot the other me had been standing. Dropped down to the thin, beige carpet and felt around for any sign

I'd been there. Little indentations from that me's leather boots or something.

Nothing.

But then, it *was* just rental carpet. Not exactly shaggy.

I shook my head.

No. It was nothing. Had to be nothing. No way I actually saw myself standing there. Just woke up a little slow from a bad dream. That was all.

But I was awake. And from the way my heart was pounding, I knew I wouldn't get back to sleep anytime soon.

I grabbed my thin red robe from the back of the bedroom door and shrugged it over my skinny shoulders. I needed to work out more. Give the girls more muscles to look at when I was on stage. The other guys in the band all said so.

I flexed my skinny arm into an unimpressive muscle, sighed, and wandered across the hall into my songwriting studio. I was awake anyway. Figured I'd pick up my guitar and work on a track or two for the next album until I relaxed enough to go back to sleep.

I got to the doorway of my home studio and saw myself standing in the middle of the room.

My home studio was the second, smaller bedroom of my little apartment. Made it even smaller with foam baffling on the walls and ceiling. Just big enough for my laptop, my six channel Mackie mixer, my three guitars on stands – a Gibson semi-electric, a Fender Jaguar, and an Ovation acoustic – my Shure SM58 microphone set up and ready to go, and a roller chair for me to sit in.

The room smelled like Nag Champa incense. Helped me concentrate when I wrote songs.

But the me in the room wasn't sitting in the chair, and he wasn't writing songs or lighting incense.

He was standing there, staring at me. Just like the first one.

Exactly like the first one. Frozen in a moment. Not even the rise and fall of his chest as I stared at him. Like a video, hung while load-ing, not yet able to play.

That me was even dressed the same way as the first one. "The End" tour shirt and my favorite jeans. Unshaven, and he hadn't washed his hair that day. Today? Couldn't tell. Made me reflexively rub my face, feel my own growth coming in all too fast.

And that me had the same worried expression on his face.

I took a step forward and just like that, life. He was breathing. His eyes darted over me.

"Am I the first one?" he said, hope in his voice.

"No," I said, while my guts were starting to clench up at the weird-ness of it all, and my nuts started threatening to tuck themselves up inside my body for safe keeping. But I still managed to jerk a thumb back toward the bedroom and say, "There was another when I woke up, and—"

"Crap! Then it may be too late already."

I started to ask a question, but that me held up a hand for silence, and I wasn't sure I should argue the point. He might pop any moment.

"Get over to Sally's place. Pronto dente. Otherwise—"

And he popped.

COVERED IN SWEAT NOW, AND MY STOMACH ROILING LIKE SOMEONE HAD snuck guacamole into my midnight burrito, I went running back into my room, fast enough that my robe flared out behind me.

I threw my robe on my bed. Grabbed the first clothes I could get out of my drawers, yanked them on. Followed them with my favorite black leather boots – the ones that went most of the way to my knees and made me look badass – and started hustling for the door.

Sally might be surprised to have me knocking on her door at four-thirty in the morning, but I knew she'd let me in. If only because she'd want the booty call.

I paused in the kitchen to make sure Max, my white tabby, had food, then grabbed my keys off the ring on the fridge, my leather motorcycle jacket and helmet off the back of my front door into the cold night air, and hustled down the stairs, shrugging both of them on as I went.

My boots clanged the wrought iron supports of the concrete slab steps as I rushed down...

...and almost ran into the third me. This one had his hair tied back, my motorcycle jacket on, and my helmet in his hands.

Same shirt and jeans. Guess I knew what I grabbed from my drawers then.

"Hurry," this me said, "and when you get there, don't start angry. Hear her out before you—"

Then that me popped.

Man, that knot in my gut wasn't getting any better with these half-assed warnings. I hoped the next me had time to finish a damned sentence.

I hustled to my parking spot, where my Harley was waiting. Sans another me, which was some small wonder.

I fired it up and hit the streets. Trying to remind myself to stay calm, no matter how much sweat was dripping down my back. No matter how tight my guts and shoulders were. How fast my heart was pounding.

My mouth was dry, and I could still taste the remains of that burrito. Made me wish I'd had another. Might have settled my stomach.

The streets of Sunnyvale were quiet after four in the morning. Empty enough that I could scoot around any cars in my way as I weaved down through side streets to Sally's place.

Sally had a house. Rented one with three of her friends. All of them hot, but only Sally liked my band. Pity. A house full of groupies would have had possibilities.

I suppose it said something about me that I could think that way, even after three mes had tried to warn me and get me going to prevent something that sounded important, even if they never quite managed to tell me what it was.

But then, that kind of libido was pretty much a job requirement for me.

I pulled up outside Sally's place, on a suburban street so quiet even the dogs were asleep at this hour. I parked out front, but had to park three doors down. For some reason, the curb in front of Sally's place was crowded with cars.

Sally threw a party and didn't invite me? Is that what the other me was trying to warn me about? Not exactly something that would piss me off. She and I weren't exclusive or anything...

I shook my head and hot-footed it over to Sally's place.

Curtains were drawn in the windows of her two-story place. Looked storybook. Lemon yellow paint, with creamy white trim. Front lawn mown down to a few scant inches. Sunflowers growing under the windows. A pink flamingo in the middle of the lawn, that someone had fitted a tiny top hat onto.

As I went up the walk, I could tell there *were* lights inside. Not her lamps, but dim light. Flashlights, maybe. And I didn't hear party sounds as I stepped onto the porch. Wiped my boots on her "Get Bent" welcome mat.

I paused before knocking. Tried to figure out what I was going to say. *Hi, Sally. Sorry to trouble you, but three different versions of myself insisted I get right over here.*

I snorted and shook my head. I wouldn't give a reason. I'd just...

What was that?

I listened a little closer. Heard what sounded like chanting...

Oh, man. If Sally was having an *orgy* and didn't invite me, then I *would* be pissed.

I knocked on the door, my usual seven-beat knock: three, three, one.

I HAD TO KNOCK TWICE BEFORE THE DOOR OPENED, CARRYING WITH IT the scent of some kind of incense I didn't recognize. Heavy stuff. Pungent.

It was Marsha, one of Sally's roommates. The brunette with short hair, an impressive figure, and a smile that looked like an invitation.

She wasn't smiling now. And she was wearing a robe. I don't mean a bathrobe. I mean a black, silk robe with a hood, like she was guest-starring in some television episode as Satanist Number Three.

"What are you doing here, Holland?" she hissed.

I could hear chanting louder now. Wasn't able to pick out the words. Didn't sound like English. Simple rhyme scheme though, and the scansion could have come from Mother Goose.

And over the chanting, the distinctive sound of Sally's breathless sex moans.

"You *are* having an orgy," I said, astonished and pissed, and not hiding it in my voice. "Sounds like I'm not too late to join in though."

Marsha tried to say something, but I grabbed her and kissed her.

Marsha blinked surprise, but she'd had the hots for me for months, and we both knew it. She was always teasing me that some-time I'd come over to see Sally and never make it to Sally's bedroom.

Marsha's arms went right around me, one hand to my butt. She kissed me with as much enthusiasm as I kissed her. Maybe more.

When I pulled back from the kiss, I gave her a smoldering smile that had nothing to do with the anger in my gut at being excluded, and whispered, "Looks like tonight's the night for us, Marsh. Make sure you save some for me."

I set her back on her feet and stepped past her.

"Wait," she said, one hand trying to grab my shoulder, but I slipped it.

I strode into the living room...

...and onto what looked like the set of a movie.

All the furniture was gone. The big throw rug too. About a dozen people in black robes, stood around a red pentagram, painted onto the hardwood floor, and marked at the corners with black pillar candles. The source of the incense was a censer near the apex of the pentagram, just outside the circle, issuing enough smoke to give the whole room a slight haze.

In the middle of that pentagram was Sally. Beautiful and blonde as ever. Naked as I'd seen her many times, flat on her back, and giving it up to Cliff, my bassist, just as naked, and who didn't have any better rhythm at sex than he had on the bass, from the look of things.

What a bastard! Yeah, Sally and I weren't exclusive, but that just meant she could date and sleep with other guys. My band mates were off-limits to her, same as her roommates were off-limits to me, outside of an orgy.

So having an orgy and inviting Cliff and not inviting me?

And Cliff accepting the invitation?

And Cliff banging *my* groupie?

Oh, this had to stop and I meant *right this second.*

I pushed past the black-robed people, and shoved at Cliff's butt with my boot.

"Get the fuck off her, Cliff," I said, "before you bore her to sleep."

The chanting stopped, and worried mumbling replaced it. Sally looked up at me, dazed a little maybe, like there was some pot mixed in with the incense or something. If there was, I was going to kick Cliff's ass even harder than I already intended to.

Our band had a strict no drugs policy.

Sally blinked at me. "Holland?"

"Dude! No!" I knew that voice from behind me. Randal, our drummer. He had to be the one who just grabbed my shoulders.

"Fuck you, Randal," I said and snapped my bootheel up between his legs.

He let go. Doubled over. I shoved him back with my boot.

"You idiot," Cliff said. "If you stop the ceremony—"

He might have had more to say, but I kicked him in the face.

Just a kick though. Not a stomp. Only hard enough to shut him up, not stop him from singing backup at our gig next week. Might not have even chipped a tooth, though I hoped I did. Would have served the bastard right.

"Who the fuck do you think you guys are?" I said, glaring around. I recognized every face. Not just the two members of my band – at least Douglas, our lead guitarist, had given this a pass, if they'd invited him – and Sally's roommates. Everyone else in a black robe had been to several of our concerts around the Bay Area.

"You're going to throw an orgy and not invite the star of the show?"

I turned to kick the incense.

"No!" Sally screamed. "Don't! If that stops goes out—"

I kicked the incense.

And the world went away.

BLACKNESS. BLACKNESS THAT SMELLED THICK, LIKE THAT INCENSE.

"It's called Dragon's Blood," a voice said. A deep voice, that sounded like it should have echoed, but didn't. "Though they mixed it with certain important herbs."

"Fuckers got stoned to throw an orgy," I said, shaking my head. Or at least, I thought I was shaking my head. Everything was so black I couldn't tell for sure. Felt right though. "Serves 'em right if I fucked it up for them."

Brave words, but I didn't feel them. My whole body was on lockdown, and my heart was pounding faster than Randal ever played in his life.

"Where am I, anyway?"

"Right now," the voice said, "you're nowhere. Your own fault for interrupting the ritual."

"Ritual? You mean the orgy?"

"Orgy?" The voice chuckled. "An orgy would have been good. Would have had me in a better mood when I answered their summons. Instead, it would have been a typical night for me."

"Well, what's this ritual then?" I said. Truth to tell, I felt a little better that it hadn't been an actual orgy, but Cliff was still not off the hook for banging Sally. He and I were going to have more than words over that.

Some rules just can't get broken, or all you have is anarchy.

"A ritual to summon me, of course."

"And who are you?"

The voice chuckled again. "Oh, no. You cannot have my name for free. You must earn the right to speak it."

But then the voice sounded bitter. "Even if the only ones who speak it these days do not know my truths."

Yeah, if this voice wasn't going to tell me its name, I figured it wouldn't tell me what its "truths" were either.

"So why were they summoning you?"

"The same reason all summon me. They want fame and fortune."

"Fame and..." I hadn't thought it was possible for me to get even angrier, but apparently I was wrong about that. I got so mad that even the endless blackness seemed to develop a reddish haze.

"Those bastards," I spat. "Those lazy, useless bastards. How dare they!"

"I had the impression," the voice said in sarcastic tones, "that they intended for you to benefit. You are, I believe, Holland Kuiper, the lead singer of The Raised?"

"That's me," I said with a nod, "but I'm not in a position to sign autographs right now."

That got me another chuckle. "You miss my point. You would have—"

"Yeah, yeah," I said. "Cliff was going to sell his soul or something to have the band hit the big time. Right?"

A pregnant pause before the voice said, in a considering tone, "Something like that. Do you disapprove?"

"Hell yes, I disapprove."

"Why? You could have enjoyed all the benefits, though they would have been the ones paying the price on your behalf. Assuming you stayed with the band, anyway."

"Because *fuck that!*" Every drop of anger I'd been feeling since I first thought I'd been excluded from an orgy came pouring out in my next words. "I practice day and night. I take classes on songwriting and production. Not just guitar. Not just voice lessons. I work with coaches on my stage moves. I work my tail to the bone for what I do. And I expect my bandmates to work just as hard."

Silence from the voice. But it was the strangest thing. I could almost feel the voice watching me.

Too much for me. I kept talking. Though my words sounded more bitter than angry now.

"I don't need to cheat. I don't *want* to cheat. I want to *earn* what I make. Every dollar. Every fan. I want it to be *real*."

I looked over to where I thought the voice was, even though when I heard it speak, it seemed to come from all around me. There was a place where it seemed to be concentrated, based on the being-watched feeling I kept getting.

"So thanks, but no thanks. I don't need your deal. I don't want your help. I just want a chance to prove myself. If I'm not good enough to make it without cheating, then I don't want it."

"You mean that," the voice said, more than a little amazed.

"Of course," I said.

"No," the voice said. "I mean you *truly* mean that. I hear the essence of your desires when you speak. They resonate from the core of your spirit. This is who and what I am. And what you just expressed. It is who and what you are."

I didn't know what to say to that, so I didn't.

But the voice didn't speak for a time, and the silence got to me first.

"So, yeah, even if it got me here, I'm glad I broke up their ritual. I'd rather be here than get everything I ever wanted without earning it."

"Where would you prefer to be?" the voice said. "Think of it, and tell me. Tell me with all that you are, and I will send you there. No price. You have already paid me more than you know, by showing me something I did not know a human could possess."

I didn't know exactly what the voice meant by that, but if it could send me back, I wanted to go. I wanted to go home. But I also wanted to kick Cliff's ass. And I wanted to tell Douglas what these idiots tried to do. I wanted...

All of that came rushing out at once.

"Home. No, at Sally's. No—"

And then I was out of the darkness.

I WAS HOME, ALL RIGHT. I WAS STANDING IN MY BEDROOM, LOOKING AT my sleeping self. And I was in my studio. And I was on my way to Sally's. And I was in the corner at Sally's. And I was other places too, but I couldn't parse them all yet.

I was all these places, and I could see each other them at the same time. Every one of these places overlaid itself on top of each other. Each distinct, but separate.

So were the sounds. My sleep breathing. Early larks in the parking lot trees. The chanting at Sally's house before I broke in. Cliff and Sally still in their robes. Not yet naked and fucking.

Then each of the scenes snapped and I was only in one place. The place I'd most wanted to be: home. And before that ritual happened, so I could stop it and do it right.

At least, I thought it was before the ritual. I couldn't see the clock from where I stood, and before I could move, the me in bed started waking up. Mumbled a question up at me, but I didn't have time for that me's questions.

I needed to know what he knew. I needed to know if there was still time. Unless he'd already broken it up...

Maybe he had. Maybe that me got back from Sally's place already. Depended on which me I was. If I was the first one, showing up before the ritual, then there was still time...

"Have you been there yet?" I asked my sleepy self.

A CONFUSING PERIOD OF TIME LATER, THERE WAS ONLY ONE ME LEFT. AT least, I was pretty sure there was only one me left. I know I was leaving the scene of the non-orgy and I hadn't popped yet.

I forgave most of the participants. They were fans who just

thought they were trying to help my career, and I couldn't fault them for that.

Cliff and Randal, I could fault. Those first kicks had been pretty good though. More solid than I'd thought. So maybe I wouldn't kick their asses any further. Maybe. That would depend on what they would have to say for themselves at the band meeting tomorrow night.

They were on thin ice though. I wanted achievers in my band, not people looking to grease the wheels. And I was pretty sure Douglas felt the same way. Probably why they didn't invite him either.

Sally, I wasn't sure I could forgive. She knew how I felt about cheap shortcuts, and she definitely knew our rules about who was and who wasn't off-limits in our little relationship.

I told her I'd think about it.

And I left with Marsha on the back of motorcycle, her hands already all over me.

After all, fair was fair.

REVERSING ILL FORTUNE

REVERSING ILL FORTUNE

II:55 PM.

New Year's Eve, and Tyler Paulson finds himself in what is probably the last place anyone is supposed to be. Standing on a north-facing, rocky outcropping near the peak of Northern California's Mount Diablo.

Stupid name for the place. Nothing devilish about it. Not even a mile tall. Looks like a volcano, but isn't one. Hell, the Ohlone used to say it was the point of creation.

Looked at that way, it really should have been called Mount Angelo.

Anyway, if this is devil mountain, then Tyler must be standing on the devil's nose. And those groves of pine trees, the ones that make sure the rangers can't see him to arrest him for being here while the park is closed, those must be the devil's nose hairs.

So why is he here, instead of at Kate's party?

Two reasons, really.

First, Kate was Cheryl's sister, and there is no way Tyler can take seeing any of Cheryl's family members right now. Yeah, they're grieving too, and yeah, none of them blame him for the accident, but … he just couldn't.

But there's another reason he's standing here, under a churning sky. Bundled up and shivering against the freezing winds and periodic spits of rain. Listening to the haunted sucking sound of his propane lantern while it casts its light harsh across the gray-orange rockface. Drinking bitter coffee hot from his thermos and chewing on a chocolate cherry granola bar – Cheryl's favorite flavor, the same need for connection that made him dab a single drop of her Chanel under his nose before he came up here.

Another reason he's putting up with all of this instead of being warm and dry and hammering down bourbons at home, since he couldn't face Kate's party.

This little chunk of rock on this sad little misnamed mountain is the loneliest, most isolated spot he can think of.

And the spell said that's what he needs, if he wants to turn his life around.

And dear God in his heaven does Tyler Paulson need to turn his life around.

His luck hasn't just been bad. It's been *record-setting* bad. This past year has been the worst of his life by a longshot.

Tyler got "downsized" from three jobs this year. By December, he can't even find contract work, because the kind of coding he does has become popular – and *cheaper* – overseas.

The lack of consistent income meant he had to put his mom in a home. Dementia was starting to hit her harder, and he couldn't afford to take her in or hire help.

She still isn't talking to him. Well, when she's in a fog she doesn't remember him, so she'll talk to him, but when she returns to herself, the fury is there and Tyler gets treated to about twenty seconds of the Tone of Death before she gives him her iciest stare and dismisses him by turning away.

His kid brother Peter's no help. Can't even find him. Last Tyler heard, Peter was in Sri Lanka, but that was months ago.

Two cars died on Tyler this year.

Two.

The first one, sure, he could understand. That wonderful

Mustang was past its prime, but it was in great shape when it got murdered. Crushed to death in its sleep.

Tyler had gotten street parking downtown for a job interview – contract bullshit at a third his normal rate, but an interview at least – and returned to find out a Hummer had slammed into that poor Mustang headlong. Driven by a guy who had the kind of money that kept him from even getting a DWI, despite a blood-alcohol content that had to be measured in proof.

Yeah, the allegedly drunk driver did have tons of insurance. But Tyler loved that Mustang.

Didn't even get the job.

Anyway, Tyler did the sensible thing, since he wasn't working. Got one of those cheap new electrics and cut way the hell back on fuel and consumables.

Then came the accident.

Tyler'd been behind the wheel, going seventy-five on 280 through the curves of the beautiful, green Los Altos hills. Sun bright and cheerful on a brisk day, and Cheryl in the passenger seat.

Cheryl. Tyler's feisty five-foot firebrand. When she smiled, people a mile away felt their spirits lift, and when she raged, people twice that distant snapped at each other.

Cheryl was laughing that day. Singing the old theme song to *Speed Racer*, because Tyler was in lane three, just moving with the traffic, and it was still the fastest he'd driven his new car.

The car just … died as they came around a curve. Dashboard went dark. Pedals wouldn't respond. Nothing.

Turned out there'd been … a little "extra" solder in the wrong spot of his new car's mother board. A very *vulnerable* spot. And once the engine heated up enough...

Anyway, the *road* curved. With the power steering dead, Tyler and Cheryl went straight. Cut right across into lane four. Without a signal, of course.

Lane four, where an eight-cylinder *behemoth* was going for a land speed record in its haste to get to San Jose International.

Apparently it was a wonder that even *Tyler's* airbag deployed. Cheryl had no shot.

Yeah, there was a lawsuit underway and all that. But the car company's lawyers have been talking about how Tyler was exceeding safe speeds, the behemoth driver's lawyers have been railing about unsafe lane changes, and...

Let's face it. The way Tyler's luck has been going, he'll be the one hit with the vehicular manslaughter charge, and the car company won't end up with an ounce of liability.

Not that money would bring Cheryl back. But damn it, these people shouldn't be able to make it sound like *Tyler's* fault. They shouldn't be able to...

That is why Tyler stands here, a miserable man in a miserable place.

To turn things around. To reverse his fortunes.

He's done just what the book said. Come to the loneliest place he can think of. He's even come on the night of new beginnings.

Isn't that what the new year is all about? New beginnings? If not a clean slate, at least a chance to do things better than before?

Hell, Tyler's even come to a place that was said to be the exact spot of creation. How much more appropriate a location could he get?

So Tyler has to have done at least this part right so far.

11:56 pm.

Tyler digs the candles out of his battered old college backpack. Pillar hurricane jobbies that came with their own glass windshields. He chooses the most level spot he can find on the rock, and sets the candles around himself according to the order in the book.

White in the north, green in the east, gold in the west, purple in the south, and blue, with Tyler, in the center. Each of those candles has the right symbol carved on it, symbol facing into the circle. Tyler made sure to carve them accurately back in his apartment, with the tip of a Philip's head screwdriver. Each symbol a different combination of a circle, a triangle, and a straight line.

The candles have clashing scents, but even he doesn't expect to smell them, even after he lights them. He has the Chanel under his nose. And even if the Chanel fades, the whipping wind will probably overrun the candles with the scents of rain and pine.

He lights the candles with a long, fireplace clicker. Even with the glass protecting the wicks, he still needs three or four tries to light each candle.

Funny, that this is when the moment of doubt hits. When he's standing there, surrounded by candles on a chunk of rock that hangs off the side of Mount Diablo.

What in God's name is he doing?

Tyler falls to his knees on the hard rock. Every muscle in his body clenches down tight, like some primal urge is getting him ready to explode into fight or flight, but can't choose which, or even which direction.

His heart pounds loud enough that he hears it over the howl of the wind and the sucking of his lantern. Feels it too. Like his common sense is trapped in his chest, trying to beat its way out of his rib cage and force him to stop and think about what the fuck he's doing.

Casting a spell?

From a book he found on the internet, yet?

Hardly even a book. A freaking pamphlet thirty pages long, published by an obscure British house. Reads like it was written for a late-night infomercial.

Tyler almost packs it in right then. Almost stomps the candles under his hiking boots. Almost kicks them over the side and down into those sopping wet groves of pines.

Almost throws himself flat and cries until the stupid passes and he gets the kind of headache he deserves for thinking this could possibly work.

But Tyler remembers the reviews. The dozens of reviews. The hundreds of reviews. All the people who swore that this little book, this pamphlet, that it's the *real thing*. That the spells in this little book *actually work.*

Is Tyler desperate enough to believe that?

Even now he isn't sure.

Is he desperate enough to try it anyway?

Yes. Yes he is.

11:58 pm.

The book says that Tyler is supposed to make sure he "feels his need strongly."

Not a problem.

Tyler figures he has more desperation in his veins right now than blood. And that chocolate cherry granola bar sticking to his teeth, that's just the souring aftertaste of loss, made even more bitter by the coffee.

The howling wind, that's the railing of his soul for the loss of Cheryl.

The periodic spits of rain, those are the tears that hit him unexpectedly now and then throughout his daily life.

Even the rocky outcropping under his hiking boots, that's just the barrenness his life has become.

Does Tyler feel his need strongly?

Oh, yes.

Which means it's time to start the chant.

The words of the chant itself, as written in the book, make no sense, of course. Apparently they're from some ancient collection of magical papers that had been lost when the Library of Alexandria burned. The author claims to have recovered the magic contained in his book by contacting a particular spirit during a séance held on what he claims is the site where that famous library once stood.

The author, of course, has helpfully supplied a phonetic rendering of the chant. Complete with hints about where to put emphasis, how long to pause between words and so forth.

The words themselves are supposed to be the names and accolades of ancient, lost divine figures who will listen and respond, when the "operator" calls them properly. Tyler, in this case, being the "operator."

Tyler is supposed to complete the chant thirty times, speak his need, and receive it.

He starts his chant now. Harsh, guttural consonants interspersed with odd, flowing vowels. They're all nonsense sounds to Tyler, but he doesn't think about that. He just keeps his mind focused squarely where it's supposed to be.

Tyler needs a reversal of fortune.

So, surrounded by the right candles, in the right place, at the best time he can think of, Tyler chants.

Midnight.

Tyler finishes his chant just at his smartwatch alarm tells him it's midnight. The chant has calmed him, to his surprise. His heart still beats hard, but not so fast, and the tension singing in his muscles has eased a bit.

The wind stills. For a moment, the only sound is the suction of his lantern.

It's crazy, but Tyler feels a presence.

He doesn't see anything but the night sky, the trees down the slope, the candles... Nothing unexpected. And yet...

And yet, Tyler feels as though he's no longer alone on that little rocky outcropping. He feels as though there's a *thing* standing before him, just on the other side of that white, northern candle.

Tyler almost asks a question. But he's not supposed to ask questions. He's only supposed to speak his need and thank the spirits, then extinguish the candles.

And time is passing.

Tyler digs a scrap of paper out of his jacket pocket. He figures he has only one shot at this, and he needs to make it count. He can't ask for Cheryl back. That would be too much even for these lost gods. He could ask for luck, but even luck wouldn't be enough, would it?

Tyler's luck wouldn't help his mother, or even get her to forgive him. Wouldn't make sure the car company suffers for what they did to Cheryl. Wouldn't dig him out of the pit that is his existence now.

So Tyler spent most of the afternoon figuring out how to phrase his need when this moment came. And now that it's here, he angles that scrap of paper to the light of his lantern and speaks his need in the most succinct and complete way he can think of.

"Please. My life has gone to hell. I need to turn my life around." He bows his head. "Thank you."

The moment he finishes talking, he hears a sound in the distance. Perhaps it's merely the horn of a passing train, but it sounds more like a gong.

11:59 pm.

Tyler chants, his mouth working those harsh consonants and long vowels while his fingers track the count. He's on twenty-nine.

Wait.

He's on twenty-eight now.

What's going on here?

By the twenty-fifth chant, Tyler figures it out. Tries to stop chanting.

By the twentieth chant, he can only scream deep within his own head, as he walks his way backwards through his life.

THE NIGHT OF ABSINTHE AND REGRET

THE NIGHT OF ABSINTHE AND REGRET

NEVER THOUGHT I'D BE BREAKING INTO MY OWN APARTMENT, BUT I couldn't carry any metal with me. So no keys.

Not a problem, though. I knew which window in the back bedroom didn't quite close all the way. Caused a lot of problems keeping the bedroom warm in the winter, the way the cold air would just seep through it. Right now, though, I was grateful.

The apartment building was a converted Victorian house. Four of us had our own rooms there, and we shared a communal kitchen. I was lucky enough to have gotten the master suite, so I had my own sitting room, bathroom, walk-in closet, and enough space for my own refrigerator.

Pretty sweet setup, for the price. Even if the landlord never upgraded anything he didn't have to.

Cheap bastard never spent a dime more than the law required.

It was a warm July night, just the way I remembered it. And I remembered every detail about that night. Not just because it was – had been – only last week, but for the reason I'd been willing to volunteer to test the tachyon temporal displacer.

This was the night that Julie dumped me.

Muggy, July air. Muggy wasn't common in this little Bay Area suburb of Thousand Pines. But for some reason, we'd been having unseasonal rain this year, only not tonight. Not the night I went back to, that is. That night it just threatened all night, air so thick with want of rain that it stuck my semi-cotton jumpsuit to my body.

Whatever this material was, they just had to make it silver. Like this was some Fifties SF movie. They, being the boys upstairs who funded my little department. I think they liked the idea of time travel a little too much. Every email and text message they'd sent for the past week — or would send in the coming week, I should say – had been chock full of time travel jokes.

If I saw one more warning about attempts on Hitler's life...

Anyway, just being in the past, even only a week in the past, gave me this weird sense of déjà vu. Like an echo reverberating nonstop, all through my body. A little distracting, but nothing I couldn't handle.

After all, I was a man on a mission. And I only had another ten minutes to accomplish it.

And so I paid strict attention to all my sensory details, to try to hold myself in my current present. I could hear crickets and frogs, way more than I would have heard most summers, but just the way I remembered from that – from this, I mean – night. All that rain must have been good for them.

I could smell the fresh mown grass from next door, past the redwood privacy fence. The grass *I* stood on was greening up from all the rain, but it was still mostly crabgrass and weeds from my landlord's neglect.

Then again, that's why my back bedroom window still didn't shut right. I'd stopped complaining after the third time he'd ignored me.

The weird thing, apart from that echoey sensation I mean, was that I could taste two things at once. I could taste the last dregs of my good Puerto Rican coffee, the last cup of which I'd had no more than twenty minutes ago, by my body clock. A good fifteen minutes before they strapped me in and started the machine.

But I could also taste garlic bread, and that was wrong.

That was wrong because the me that belonged in this time actually was tasting garlic bread. It was seven-oh-three p.m., and Julie and I were at that little Italian place downtown. They'd just brought us a basket of garlic bread while we looked over the menu.

I shouldn't have been able to taste that garlic bread, not current me. I hadn't had any garlic bread in a week. Had to have been some resonance effect related to that echo sensation.

I made a mental note about it, then wiped some sweat from my forehead. This semi-cotton jumpsuit didn't breathe right for this kind of weather.

I had about nine minutes of real time before I got yanked back to the present. Way more than I—

What was that?

I could hear something from inside the apartment building. Wait. It was a Thursday. Wasn't that the night that Simone from upstairs did yoga in the backyard?

Crap. I'd forgotten.

I couldn't let her see me. I mean, even apart from this outfit, she knew I was out with Julie. Couldn't leave evidence that I'd been here.

I hustled over to the window, whipped it open, and scrambled inside to fall onto my old, creaky king-size bed.

The size was the only really good thing about that bed. It was old enough now that the springs bitched every time I rolled over on it. Had to admit though, it did make ... other activities ... sound more impressive.

I got the window closed before Simone rounded the corner. She looked great as always, a willowy redhead dressed in clingy, stretchy basic black and carrying her yoga mat. Simone could have modeled for yoga calendars. She had that kind of body and that kind of smile.

In fact, it was that smile – and let's be honest, that body – that had caused my trouble in the first place.

No time for that now.

I rolled off of the bed onto the floor, and realized I was still hearing a noise from inside the house. On this floor.

At my front door.

No. That couldn't be. I knew for a fact that Julie and I were still at the restaurant. I could taste the Italian coffee we'd ordered, and I could still taste that strong garlic bread.

So who was trying to open my front door?

I crossed the squeaky wood in two dozen quick paces, stepping over and around the piles of books and magazines I went through like a fiend, yet never managed to find room for on my many book-shelves.

Probably because I needed more bookshelves, but I was out of wall space.

I got to my front door, and picked up my baseball bat from the umbrella stand…

And immediately dropped it.

I couldn't hit someone who came in. Could I? I mean, they had to have actually come in last time, didn't they?

Or, wait, the last time was this time, wasn't it? I mean, this is a week ago, which means that last week, while I was at the restaurant with Julie, I was actually here, wasn't I?

Wait, if that were true, then this whole mission was doomed to failure.

I dove to the other side of my oversized, overstuffed brown couch and hid. I needed time to figure this out, and I didn't have it. I was down under eight minutes now, and someone was working the knob of my door like they had a key or could pick the lock.

I needed to think.

Last week – I mean tonight – Julie had come home with me after our date. Nothing special in and of itself, except that any night with Julie was special. No, the problem didn't come until later that night. When Julie had gone to the bathroom, and found Simone's panties down on the floor, behind my garbage can.

If I'd only remembered to take my garbage out a few days ago, I could have thrown them out with the garbage, and Julie would never have known about my drunken dalliance with Simone. She'd never have dumped me.

It was all so stupid. Simone wasn't into me. I wasn't into her. But she had that bottle of absinthe, and we'd both always wanted to try it.

And a drink became four, and then we were laughing at every little thing, and then she started showing me yoga poses, and then...

Well, her panties did end up on my bathroom floor. Strange that she didn't think to find them.

Come to think of it, if I'd traveled a few days further, I could have just taken out the garbage, and...

No. The warning signs were all there in the math that I'd gone over with the team at least a dozen times while prepping for this trip. No more than a week exactly into the past. Which meant tonight. Which meant while Julie and I were at the restaurant. No leaving evidence that I'd been there, which meant I couldn't have taken out the garbage, even if I did at least grab those panties.

Whoever was at the knob started knocking.

I blinked in confusion then. If they had the key, why would they...

I smacked myself in the forehead. Someone had the wrong room.

I moved up to the door and, gruffing my voice down a half an octave, said, "What?"

"I'm looking for Andrew?"

"Three C, across the hall."

"Thanks."

I could hear shoes moving away.

Six minutes.

I scrambled for the bathroom then. Found those pink, French-cut panties, zipped down my jumpsuit, and tucked them into my own underwear.

Couldn't afford a bulge in any pocket. Someone might notice and ask, and nothing good would result from that.

But I had to have something else to bring back with me. Some piece of evidence that I'd been here, and that proved I could carry something back with me through time.

I debated this longer than I'm proud of. I'd been so focused on finding those panties that I hadn't thought about the official reason for the mission, and what I'd need.

I almost grabbed a dozen things. My toothbrush. Used dental floss. A slice of bread.

In the end, I grabbed a dirty sock from out of my laundry. I might have noticed my toothbrush or some food going missing – and nobody would want to preserve my used dental floss for posterity as evidence of our success at time travel – but no way I'd notice a missing sock.

Like any sane person, I'd assume it was eaten by the washing machine.

I'd just stuffed the sock into the pocket of my jumpsuit when the time travel sensation overtook me.

Time travel was unlike anything else I'd ever experienced, and I'd trained as an astronaut.

The sensation began with floating. Not just in my gut, where I usually noticed that kind of kinetic sensation, but all through my torso, from, well, my bottom end all the way through my collarbone.

Then my head felt compressed, like when my big brother used to get me in a headlock and I managed to keep the pressure off my neck. It was that same squeezing from the sides.

But that wasn't just my head, getting squeezed that way. My hands and feet too. As though all my most distant parts got slowly crushed.

Then the squeezing moved inward, up my legs and arms, down my neck and shoulders, until every part of me felt compressed. As though time were a giant snake, trying to digest me.

All of this, while still getting that floating, weightless sensation.

But once those two sensations came together, then it got really weird.

For an instant, I could see everything. I mean everything. It was like every single thing around me was still connected to every single thing it had ever been and would ever be. I could see the flames that would consume this building someday. I saw the forest that once stood on this spot, and every tree connected to every board and every plank of wood ever to come into this building. Every cotton shrub that produced the clothes worn here, and everyplace those clothes would go, and every person who would wear them.

All of it. And so very much more.

Overwhelming.

I blacked out again. Just the way I had while traveling backward.

BUT THAT WAS THE THING ABOUT TIME TRAVEL. THAT BLACKOUT MIGHT have lasted a year and a day, as far as my body was concerned. Only the doctors would be able to figure that out after I got back to my own time.

But in the moment, that blackout took exactly zero time.

It was as though the whole process, from the first hints of floating and compression through that instant of omniscience and my blacking out, all happened in less than a blink of my eyes.

At the end of that blink, I was still strapped to the white table, the I.V. tube still in my arm as though my body had never gone anywhere.

All around me, my team. Four of the best quantum physicists every assembled. Hyun Lee over working the keyboard of the temporal asymptote adjuster. Zamir, calibrating the tachyon relays with those four joysticks. Dottie, her pen light contrasting sharply with the dark skin of her hand, staring intently at my pupils. And Rodrigo, our team leader, overseeing the whole thing and checking everyone's work.

"He's here all right," Dottie said, her slow southern drawl making those words feel as though they took forever. Or maybe it was just an aftereffect of the time travel. "Like he's never been away."

"Better be here," Zamir said, and Hyun Lee echoed the sentiment. Zamir continued, "All readings show the drop and spike that correspond with our predictions."

"Yes," Hyun Lee added. "Everything has responded as though it worked perfectly."

"Well," Rodrigo said, giving me that slow smile of his. "Did you make it?"

"Yep. Right to my backyard, just the way we planned it."

That got everyone over to the table. Dottie and Zamir got the straps undone while Rodrigo popped my I.V. out and slapped a band-aid on the puncture point.

"Well?"

I'm pretty sure everyone asked that question at the same time.

I slowly stuck my hand into my pocket, ready for the big, dramatic reveal.

But my pocket was empty.

They must have seen it in my face. Or maybe in the way I was digging around in the pocket of my silver semi-cotton jumpsuit.

They all looked crestfallen.

"No," I said, sitting up. "I was there. I swear it. There was even a resonance effect we hadn't planned on. I could taste what I was having for dinner. I mean the me that lived through last week. His dinner. I could taste it from my backyard."

"And what did you try to bring back?" Rodrigo said, not trying to disguise the disappointment in his voice, but maybe holding out just a little hope.

"A dirty sock."

That got a general rumble of agreement about my choice.

"Oh, well," Rodrigo said. "We'll have to write this off as a failure and start troubleshooting what went wrong."

"No!" I jumped to my feet then on the black and white tile floor. "I'm telling you I was there. I saw Simone come into the backyard to do her yoga."

That got a snicker out of Zamir, but that was only because he'd met Simone a couple of times when he'd come over for a beer. Not because he had any idea about the night of absinthe and regret.

"There to watch, her, huh?" he said.

"No! It was as far back as we could send me. I just wanted to slip in through my back window and grab a sock and…"

"Doesn't matter," Hyun Lee said. "It's not evidence. Zamir already told us that Simone does yoga in the backyard every Thursday."

"Why do you think I always want to come over for a drink on Thursdays?" Zamir bobbed his eyebrows.

I shook my head. The team started to shut down the equipment.

"Wait!" I said.

"Just put it in your report," Rodrigo said. "We might be able to get some value out of your experience, at least, even if it was illusory."

"No! Wait!" Maybe it was the urgency of my tone, but they all turned and looked back at me. "My neighbor. Andrew. He had a visitor that night who tried to knock on my door. If I can confirm that – and I hadn't known it before – then that's new information I could only have gained by going backwards in time."

"Thin," Hyun Lee said.

"Too thin," Dottie added. "No way for us to prove you didn't already know."

"I spoke to him. The visitor."

"What?" Rodrigo's voice came out so sharp I half expected he'd cut my cheek.

"Through my front door. He'd tried to open it. He never saw me. And I gruffed up my voice so it didn't sound like me."

Rodrigo bobbed his head back and forth while he thought about that.

"Zamir," he said, "you go over to Jason's for a drink on Thursdays, right?"

Zamir nodded. "Not every Thursday, but yeah."

"So you have an excuse to be there. You ask the neighbor about it. Record the conversation. Video, if you can sneak it."

"Not legal," Dottie said in a sing-song tone.

"It's not evidence in court," Rodrigo said. "We just need proof for our records."

The two of them began to argue about that, while Hyun Lee and Zamir pressed me for everything I could remember about the trip through time. From the physical sensations, to the odd déjà vu bit, to the co-locative sense of taste and more. Everything I could remember.

Everything I admitted to remembering anyway. Because I could remember that night full well. Both my recent trip back, and the night I'd lived through.

I'd moved through time and space to try to spare Julie that discovery. Maybe I was being selfish, trying to keep Julie as my girlfriend even though I'd cheated, but I didn't see it that way. I saw it as trying to make up for one night's mistake. To save our relationship.

Didn't matter which way I thought of it though.

I failed to steal the panties from the past.

Julie found them that night. Knew they weren't hers.

We still had that fight.

Julie still dumped me.

Everything happened just the way I remembered it.

TRAPPED IN SEPIA

TRAPPED IN SEPIA

The moment before the car would hit me seemed to take forever.

I was turning my head as I stepped off the curb, and there it was. Cherry red '88 Corvette Stingray, front fender heading straight for my knees from a distance of maybe twenty feet.

The world seemed to hold its breath.

The sudden roar of the engine, stilled. The singing of bluebirds in those nearby maple trees too. Chattering from pedestrians on the sidewalk nearby – and there were dozens on this block alone. This part of downtown Portland was always crowded at noontime.

My eyes were fixed on that car though. The bumper. Even the license plate: G44281F. Oregon plate. Wouldn't expire for another two years. Just renewed this month. July.

Couldn't see who was behind the wheel. Not with my eyes on the bumper. Pristine red bumper. Even had a fleeting thought, wondering if it would still be pristine when it clipped me. If my bones were hard enough to crack the fiberglass. If my own blood would look darker against the yellowish red of the car.

I couldn't even feel the July heat on my skin. Not in that instant.

And it was a sunny day in Portland, during one of the few months when we could count on more sun than rain.

I was supposed to be meeting my girlfriend Adela for coffee in five minutes.

I had the feeling I wasn't going to make it.

All of that, every bit of it, all in a single instant. A single, *sharp* instant. I was keenly aware of crumbs between my teeth from my morning English muffin. The hints of butter still on my tongue. The beads of sweat under the collar of my pale blue tee shirt.

Adela's favorite color on me. She said it brought out my eyes.

Wouldn't be this color much longer.

Then it occurred to me that something strange was going on. I could think. I could draw conclusions, or at least questions, about my shirt and the car and whether or not I'd make it to see my girlfriend. Even enough to wonder how long she'd have to wait before someone called her for me from the hospital.

But if I could think, then time had to be passing. Didn't it? I couldn't very well think, while literally frozen. Thoughts were electrical impulses in the brain, weren't they? And those impulses, if they fired then time was passing.

"Very good," an echoing voice said. Deep and rumbly, but for the life of me I couldn't tell where it was coming from.

Two quick things occurred to me, in succession.

One, I was definitely hearing that with my ears, and if sound could carry impulses to my brain, then time was definitely moving. Somehow.

Two, I had no idea who was talking, or where they were.

But those things didn't matter to me. Not in that single moment of almost-frozen time.

If impulses could carry thoughts through my brain and sound through my ears, then they could carry orders to my muscles.

I screamed at my muscles to dive back onto the crosswalk.

A moment ago – if it could have been a moment ago – I'd tried to look at the driver of the car, but my eyes hadn't moved. Neither had my head.

Now though, presumably in the same instant, my body obeyed and I dove onto the sidewalk.

Time started the instant my body moved.

The corvette whipped past, it's breeze hitting my back as I plunged back onto the sidewalk...

...and right into a man in a navy blue suit who looked uncomfortably like my father. Same steel gray hair at the same short length. Same softening build. Same disapproving brown eyes.

Though in his defense, that might have been because I was mid tackle.

Down we went. He cushioned my fall, but I didn't think thanking him was the right move.

"Sorry," I said, extricating myself from his inadvertent embrace, and reaching for the brown alligator briefcase I'd dislodged from his hand.

I stayed on my knees as I handed it back to him.

"Don't worry about it," he said, the disapproval in his eyes turning to follow the escaping Corvette, just as a cop car down the block hit its siren and took off after the reckless driver. "Are you all right?"

"Me?" I said, standing now and helping him up. "Better than I was about to be."

I released his hand, and the world went all sepia toned. The man continued talking, but his words faded to incoherence. So did the sounds of the pedestrians around me, most of them going on about their day, footsteps muted on the sidewalk, their words so muffled they might have been on the other side of three layers of sheetrock.

The heat of the day was muted too, and the sweat on my torso and neck gelled.

My heart lurched. It had kicked up to full speed a moment before, but now it dropped from full speed to slow and casual in the space of a beat, which shook my whole body. My heart had never done anything like that before, and I was pretty sure it wasn't supposed to happen.

"A lot of things aren't supposed to happen," that voice said. It still sounded deep and gruff, but it lost its echo now. And I could tell it was coming from behind me.

I turned around, and, well, I knew I was looking at a wizard. Maybe a god, but most likely a wizard. Or at least, I was looking at what I thought a wizard should look like in this day and age.

He stood a little over six feet tall, which made him my height. And he was dressed just as casually. Tie-dyed Grateful Dead tee shirt, and worn-looking jeans that might have been old enough to have gotten grass stains at Woodstock. The man had long gray hair, like steel wool, bound six times into a bushy ponytail that went most of the way down his back. His cragged face had no beard. He wore ancient-looking Birkenstocks.

And he wasn't sepia-toned, any more than I was. His skin was tanned so deep, he might have slept outside his whole long life.

But his eyes. His eyes were blue-green and sparkled like lightning was rolling just behind them, peeking out every so often.

His thin lips smiled. He seemed to be waiting.

"Like me getting out of the way of that car?"

"Just so," he said. Still that sense of waiting.

I looked around at all the people and cars around us, going about their days. Businesspeople on their way to meetings or lunches. Tourists gawking at the occasional small statues that dotted the west side of Portland, sprinkled here and there among the buildings and sidewalks like Easter eggs. Students, with their backpacks and trendy clothes and urgent need to do everything right this very second.

And all of them sepia-toned and muffled into near silence.

The whole world was like that, except for me and this wizard. Or whatever he was.

"Like the whole world going sepia-toned?" I asked.

"Is that what's happening?"

Answering a question with a question. That settled wrong in my gut. One of those things my mom drilled into my head as rude, when I was growing up.

"Well, if you don't know..." I said and I let the words trail off as I turned away. Maybe he'd give with the information. Maybe he'd undo whatever he'd done. I wasn't sure, but I expected some kind of response from him.

"Am I the one who doesn't know?" he said.

I swore.

I turned back around in time to watch a great big, black-though-sepia-toned, shaggy Newfoundland dog walk straight through the wizard. Or whatever he was.

I blinked so fast he strobed on me for a moment.

"What about dogs walking through you? Is that supposed to happen?"

"You tell me," he said.

"NO!"

My heart steadfastly refused to speed up, even though I felt anger trying to course through my body. But without the accelerated heart rate, my adrenals weren't kicking in their share, and none of my muscles tightened up the way they were supposed to.

I wasn't sure what I wanted to do with my anger, but it was mine and I had a right to it.

"You're doing this to me, aren't you." I didn't make it a question, just to break the pattern.

He kept the pattern going anyway.

"Am I the one who's doing it?"

"Doing *what*?"

"That's the question, isn't it?" He lifted his legs to sit cross-legged right in mid-air.

He smiled at me.

"What are you?" I asked.

That broadened his smile. "Does it matter?"

I stopped. Forced myself to breathe faster and clench my fists, just because they were signs of anger I could control. The autonomic parts of my system didn't pick up the clues though.

"What happened back there? With the Corvette?"

"You're asking me?"

I nodded.

"I'd say you jumped in the nick of time. Is that what you'd say?"

I bit back my first three responses.

"Look," I said. "If you aren't actually going to tell me anything, why don't you just undo whatever you did and I'll be on my way."

He chuckled. "You're missing the point, lad." He twirled his finger to indicate the distant, sepia-toned world. "I'm not doing this."

I SHOOK MY HEAD. HARD. CLOSED MY EYES AND SPUN AROUND THERE ON the sidewalk.

Opened my eyes again, and the world was still sepia-toned and muffled. Pedestrians made their way past me as though I weren't there. Worse than that, one of them – a skinny goth girl probably not old enough to vote – walked straight through me without the slightest hesitation.

And I didn't feel her pass through me.

I looked back at the old man in his Grateful Dead getup. This maybe-wizard.

He and I were the only two things in the world in full, living color.

Though I had the distinct feeling that "living" was the wrong word.

"I'm dead, aren't I?" I said, my tone flat. "That Corvette hit me, and you're Death here to bring me to the afterlife, once I accept that I'm dead."

"Interesting theory," he said. "If that's so, then your body should be splattered on the ground over there at the corner of the block. Shall we go look?"

It was only a half-dozen paces away. I could see the area from where I stood.

No corpse. No blood-spattered Corvette. No vomiting witnesses. None of the things I might have expected to see, if I were dead.

"Let me guess," I said. "I can't see my own body because some part of me is clinging to life?"

"Now you're stretching. Come on. You've come this far. What can you figure out?"

"Come this far?"

The urge to slap this man got me as far as raising my hand, but without the proper responses from my body, I had trouble generating enough anger or even irritation to make myself strike him.

Even when he nodded encouragingly.

"All right," I said instead. "You seem to be implying that I'm the one keeping us here."

"Bringing us here," he said. "And keeping you here. Very good."

"Wait." I blinked at him. "So you can go back to the regular world anytime you want?"

"Of course." He smiled again. "But that would be leaving you here alone, and I don't think you should be alone right now. Not while you're just figuring things out."

"Figuring what out?"

"See what I mean?"

I screamed then. But nobody around me noticed except for this maybe-wizard.

"Are you a wizard?" I asked him.

"That's one word for me. Good as any other."

"Well," I said, "does that mean I'm a wizard too?"

"You might be." He nodded his head back and forth, as though assessing probabilities. "Right now I'd say it's better than even money that you will be. First, though, you have to survive."

"Survive?" I blinked fast again. Honestly, I think I was still trying to push my body for a physical reaction that it just was not going to give me. "What, dodging the Corvette wasn't enough?"

"The Corvette was impressive," he said, nodding. "Almost nobody walking this earth could have done that. Stepped outside of time. Well..." He scratched at his chin. "Far enough outside, anyway. Far enough outside to save your own life."

"Well, then what more do you want from me?"

"It's not me, lad."

"My name is Kevin."

"Then it's not me, Kevin." He shook his head, and pointed at my feet. "And that's what I'm talking about."

My feet had turned sepia-toned. And I'd never felt the difference.

<hr />

I MUST HAVE WASTED FIVE OR TEN MINUTES — IF TIME WAS PASSING, AND to judge by the pedestrians moving past me, it was — just stomping my feet and bouncing around. Trying to get some sense of difference between my feet and my ankles.

My ankles looked normal, under their white athletic socks. My feet, and their blue Nike sneakers, looked sepia-toned.

But they felt normal.

So far.

Finally, I looked up at the wizard. (He said it was a good enough term, and I was getting tired of hemming and hawing about it.)

He looked back at me, interested.

"What's going on?" I asked. "Am I easing my way back into the normal world? Will I get there on my own if I don't do anything?"

He pursed his lips, and scratched at his chin, his bushy eyebrows down as though disappointed.

"You don't really believe that, do you?" His nostrils flared in a deep breath. "I mean, you've come so far. Don't backslide to your own death."

"Death? What do you mean death?"

"It's like this." He set his feet back on the ground and began pacing back and forth through pedestrians.

And God help me, it was starting to look normal for him to do that.

"You managed to manifest an effect when your life was on the line. Almost nobody walking this earth could have done what you did. It was big enough that I felt it from Seattle."

"You were in Seattle a moment ago?"

"Think," he said, pausing in his pacing. "Did you notice me before the Corvette?"

"No."

"Would you have noticed me?" he gestured to his Grateful Dead ensemble.

I nodded.

"So you knew I wasn't here a moment ago, but I am now."

"And you came all the way from Seattle? How? Teleported?"

"Something like that. If you survive this, I'll help you figure that out. It'll help you get to your date on time."

I screamed again. Purely intellectual frustration, since my body wouldn't cooperate, but I had to vent it somehow. I was missing my date. I had to be.

He waited for me to finish the scream, and then for me to finish the panting breaths I thought I ought to do, even though I didn't strictly need them.

"Bad habit, you know," he said. "Making your body do things it doesn't need to that way. It'll cost you down the line."

"If I survive."

He nodded, then pulled his feet up and sat cross-legged again.

"Now," he said, "I was pointing out that you managed to save yourself from the Corvette by manifesting a rare talent. But the problem with that talent is that you have to embrace it. You've awakened it, but if you don't control it now, it'll unravel and undo what you did."

"You mean the Corvette could still hit me?"

"Yep. And trust me, Kevin, it'll kill you. Not immediately." His blue-green eyes gazed off into the distance. "You'll lose consciousness after an incredibly painful moment, but you'll suffer brain damage when you bounce off the hood, and again when you hit the concrete. Then there's the garbage truck."

"Garbage truck?"

"You didn't notice it." He gave me a wistful smile. "So many common things become background in our lives. We don't give them their proper due or respect."

"Can we get back to the part when I'm hitting the garbage truck?"

"Well, it hits you, really. It's stopping at the time, which is something, but the third time's the charm, as it were. Your brain can't take all the trauma. Straight into a coma. You finally pass three days from now."

"How do you know this?"

"The same way I felt the ripples of what you did, even from Seattle. The same way I got here. Which is the same way you have so far avoided the Corvette, and the same way you brought us to the place that you see as sepia-toned."

"How do you see it?"

"Green-tinted, like some 60s movies were."

"How do I stop it?" I said, waving my hand at the sepia tone that had crept past my sneakers and halfway up my jean-covered calves.

"That's the trick, isn't it? You need to figure out how to handle what's going on. How to get yourself back to the normal world on your own terms."

"And then you'll show me how to not be late for my date?"

"Sure, but I probably won't have to. Pull this off, and slipping a few minutes through time will be easy enough, because since you spent that actual time here. Not as though you have to overcome the inertia of your body being elsewhere at the same time. Heck, you'll even get to hear the rest of the monolog from the guy you tackled, if you want to."

"Joy," I said, gazing down at my legs. "So what do I need to do?"

"It's different for everybody." He shrugged. "Sorry. You've got the power to make the right choices, but it's up to you to make them."

<hr>

I DON'T KNOW HOW LONG I PACED BACK AND FORTH, TRYING TO WILL myself back into the real world. Trying to remember the instant I saw that Corvette. Trying to recall the same feelings, the same sensations, the same urgent need to live.

But none of that was doing me a damned bit of good.

By the time I looked back at the wizard, full of questions, the sepia tone had reached my hips.

"How long do I have?" I said. "When it reaches my heart, or when it covers me completely?"

"What do you think?"

"Can't you just answer the question?"

"Only if you want to die." He twirled his finger again, taking in the whole sepia-toned world. "It's all related. All of it. If I *give* you information instead of letting you figure it out, I cut you off from the very facility you need to be able to survive this."

He smiled. "So I'm not just being a dick. Honest."

I growled then and went back to pacing.

"Sometimes it helps if you think out loud," he said. "Can't give you answers, but I might be able to help with your reasoning."

I didn't see the difference there myself, but I wasn't going to question it.

"All right. I saw the Corvette. I panicked. And then, bam! Everything stopped."

"And what does that tell you?"

"I've been trying to panic for the last half hour!"

"How's that working out for you?"

I looked over at him. Serene bastard, floating in mid-air as though he didn't have a care in the world, even though it seemed as though half the city of Portland had walked right through him.

And he was still full-color, while I was half-sepia-toned, halfway to joining the throngs of...

"Wait," I said, stopping my own pacing through people to hold up a hand that was, for now at least, still full color. "Wait. If I'm half-sepia, and the world around me is sepia, why can they still walk through me?"

"Not a great question, but it might help. What do you think?"

"Because part of me is still in color?"

"Could be." He wiggled his hand in a half-and-half gesture. "You'd be better served to think more about the Corvette though."

"Wait. You mean I'm getting close?"

"You're all over the place." He smiled and shook his head. "Not your fault, though. This isn't easy to go through."

"Right." I crouched there on the sidewalk, then jumped up and ran over to the spot where the Corvette might yet still kill me. The wizard spun in the air and floated after me.

Right now a delivery truck was pulling past, and about twenty people were waiting to cross the street.

It looked perfectly normal, apart from the coloring. I didn't see what I could learn from this.

"Think," the wizard whispered. "The Corvette came at you. Then what?"

"I panicked," I said without turning around, as though the tar marks on the asphalt held answers for me. "I told you."

"And what does that tell you?"

"I don't know."

"So *think*."

Wow. The wizard was starting to lose patience with me. That couldn't be a good sign.

I glanced down and saw that the sepia tone was now halfway up my chest. And that was an even worse sign. If I'd panicked when the Corvette came at me, I should be panicking now too, by all rights.

And yet my heart rate wouldn't pick up. My breathing only changed when I thought about it.

"Wait," I said again. "You said I shouldn't force my body to have reactions it doesn't want to have."

"No," he said patiently, "I said it's a bad habit to get into."

His eyes showed more of the lightning flashing behind their blue-green color. He was trying to tell me something.

"But why would that be?" I asked, trying to will him to answer the question.

I might as well have been willing the tar on the asphalt to stand up and recite a Monty Python routine.

"Bad habit..." I crouched down. Looked over at where I'd tackled the guy who'd looked uncomfortably like my father. No answers there either.

"Bad habits are out of control, aren't they? They're things you do whether you want to or not. Aren't they?"

"That's a good definition of them," he said, smiling as he nodded from his seat three feet in the air.

"Can they cause things to happen when you don't want them to?"

He shrugged. Not getting an answer that easily then.

I smacked my forehead. That had to be the answer. It had to be.

I had to make myself panic.

But how?

I'd already tried to make my body react, and gotten nowhere with it.

But maybe I hadn't tried hard enough. Hadn't found the right angle.

I started pushing myself to hyperventilate. Breathing just as fast as I could, while pumping my fists and trying to imagine all the worst things I could think of.

Adela dumping me. No, Adela sleeping with my roommate, then dumping me, on the day I get fired from my job at...

"No!" The wizard said.

His word came out so sharp the whole train of thought got kicked out of my head.

"Sorry," he said, "but thoughts aren't the answer here. Not like that. Intentions are better. Those kind of thoughts, in a place like this, well, they could have unintended consequences." He smiled. "Wouldn't want to survive this just to get fired and lose your girlfriend and roommate on the same day."

"That could happen?"

"Priorities," he said, pointing at the sepia tone, which had reached my collarbone.

"What then?" I implored him.

He could only give me a grim smile and shake his head.

I started pushing to hyperventilate again. I started thinking about death. About the Corvette, bearing down on me. How I was too young to die. How I had so much more to do with life. How badly I wanted to live.

But, and this is the weird part, none of those were thoughts. They weren't words of an inner monolog, the way I'm used to noticing when I notice myself thinking. Instead, it was as though I was thinking my feelings. Not those good, visceral reactions I was used to from life, boiling up out of my body and bringing my hormones and autonomic responses with it.

These were purely intellectual feelings, because my body wasn't giving me the feedback I was used to. But they were all I had.

So I just kept feeding those intellectual feelings through my system, while pumping my muscles and pushing my breathing and trying to imagine myself surviving that dive for cover. Imagining the way my heart had been racing. The sound of my blood rushing past my ears. The hit in my gut from the look of disapproval in the suited man's eyes, so similar to the same look from my father.

I cut out thinking about the sepia tone. I cut out thinking about the wizard. About anything but the visceral reactions I should have been having to my close brush with death. Not my death, but my close brush with it.

"Yes," I heard the wizard murmur, but I paid him no mind.

Close brush with death. Survival. My heart pounding not with fear, but joy at survival. My limbs all twitching in celebration. My body clenching down low as important parts of myself reminded me that they were there, that they'd survived too.

I closed my eyes, grateful and excited and looking forward to telling Adela all about the reckless driver in his Corvette Stingray. The man who almost killed me.

Suddenly I could hear the suit man again.

"Honestly," the man said. "That may have been an Oregon plate, but that's pure Southern California driving. Probably wouldn't have been the first man he hit. Probably has hit-and-run charges waiting for him in three states."

I opened my eyes.

The world was in color again!

I smiled and hugged that suited man, to his intense discomfort. Apparently sympathizing with my near squashing didn't entitle me to take personal liberties with his person.

But he didn't shove me away. Just accepted his hug and hurried off the moment I let him go.

I didn't care. I smiled at the world all around me, even the pretty Japanese girl who looked so scared for me I almost wondered if she'd lost someone to an auto accident.

In that moment, just for a flash, I knew she had. Her cousin Kumiko. Not eighteen months ago.

I almost apologized. Almost offered condolences. But I checked myself at the last second and just settled for smiling at her. For saying, "It's all right. He missed me, and that cop's going to *nail him.*"

I knew I was right too. Even if I wasn't quite sure how I knew.

But the girl smiled back at me, and crossed the street with the change of the light. All around me, everyone was getting on with their day, as though I'd been the only one whose life had been irrevocably changed a moment ago.

"Almost," said a deep, gruff voice behind me. I turned to see the wizard, still in his Grateful Dead ensemble, though standing on his feet instead of floating in the air. "Gotta say my life changed a little bit today too."

"Oh? How so?"

"Well," he said with a slow smile. "You got yourself back, and that's good. You got yourself back to the instant you left, and that's even better. Better than I did, my first time. Gotta say though, you'll still need someone to show you the ropes, and that's gonna have to be me."

"When do we start?"

He smiled a little wider. "I like an eager student, but let's be honest here. Is that what you most want to do right now?"

I smiled back because I knew the answer, and I knew he knew the answer too.

"Have fun on your date," he said. "And don't worry. I'll find you later when you aren't busy."

He could too. I knew that. And I was pretty sure I could find him the same way.

But right now, the most important thing in the world to me was having coffee with Adela.

After all, I'd almost died trying to keep this date.

THE SIDE-EFFECT STAIRCASE

THE SIDE-EFFECT STAIRCASE

I reached the landing and saw more stairs where there weren't supposed to be any.

My first thought was that my count was off. I'd been hustling up echoey flights of old, gray concrete stairs with a cold, wrought iron handrail sliding under my palm. That awful smell in my nose the whole way. Like the concrete'd been wet so long it'd fermented.

Not much changed from floor to floor, including the cheap, humming fluorescent lights. One bulb over each set of stairs, another over each landing.

So, in theory, I might only've covered eleven flights. Might still be one turn away from my floor and my corner condo.

Problem there was that I'd been taking the stairs since I inherited my home from Grandma and Grandpa Spencer six months ago. Maybe a week before I'd gotten my first local I.T. job.

Well, not quite. I think I'd taken the elevator for the first few days. Until I got tired of waiting for that squeaky, glacial contraption and discovered that I liked the challenge of taking the stairs, instead.

I'd taken those stairs at least once a day each direction, ever since. More than once on days I went out. Far as I knew, I was the only one who lived above the eighth floor willing to tolerate the odor and dim lighting of the stairwell.

My legs knew the climb to my floor better than I did. And when I reached the landing in question that Friday evening, my legs told me we'd reached the twelfth floor and home.

And yet, that night, the landing led to one more turn. One more set of concrete stairs.

Didn't take much more than a glance was enough to confirm what my legs told me. The steel door off the landing had the fancy, wrought iron number twelve right where it was supposed to.

I was on the twelfth floor. The top floor. But suddenly there was a floor above me?

I stood there, staring at those unexpected stairs for a time, while my heartrate slowed back to normal. I didn't sweat from taking the stairs anymore. And though my breathing got faster and my heartrate kicked up a bit, it'd been a long time now since I'd last gotten home a panting mess who saw the blood vessels in his eyes with every pounding heartbeat.

My thighs and calves were singing a good song under my black, Friday cargo pants. I could handle one more flight of stairs, if I felt like it.

And I had to know.

The body's a funny thing. I'd gotten to the point that I could ascend twelve flights of stairs and be all right. But man, just one extra flight cost me more than I expected. My quads started bitching on the third stair up that last turn. My calves added their own complaints two steps later.

By the time I was three-fourths the way up that final staircase, I felt as though I'd climbed at least another eight flights. My heart was pounding hard. I was sweating through my red polo shirt. I had to wipe my black hair out of my eyes twice.

Even my arches, and the balls of my feet, started bitching.

I pushed on anyway. And as I did, I noticed something. Maybe because I was panting for breath.

Up here, the stairwell didn't smell so bad. Well, it smelled different, anyway. Kind of musty. Like I should've been knocking cobwebs out of my way as I ascended.

The light was different, too. No humming blueish fluorescence here. I didn't see any bulbs, but the ambient light was warmer. Yellowish. As though somebody hadn't gotten the message that Portland, Oregon, was against those old, inefficient, incandescent lightbulbs.

By the time I reached the landing, I felt like somebody'd entered me into a 10K without telling me. Had to stop and rest. Hands on my knees and my side against the cold gray concrete of the landing walls. Felt positively dizzy, which was ridiculous. Been *months* since I last felt dizzy after taking the stairs.

My legs were sore and shaky. I was feeling the effort in my lower back. Hell, I owned good sneakers, but my feet were sore. And that last snack I'd had at work – a simple but tasty glazed donut – felt like it was trying to come back up.

I was twenty-five years old, but I felt three times my age. And it was pissing me off. So much for my stairway workout routine.

"That's it," I said, between breaths. "Starting ... tomorrow ... I'm running ... again."

Took longer to get my wind back than I expected, too. I mean, I knew what it was like to push myself to near exhaustion. I used to do it on the basketball court, playing way too many pickup games. And when I'd started forgoing the elevator, I hadn't exactly been in primo athlete shape.

But standing there on the thirteenth landing, even when my heartrate was back to normal, I felt as though I wasn't getting enough wind back in my lungs. As though maybe the air was thinner here than it should've been...

That was it. Back in college I'd let my friend Ethan drag me up Mount Hood. The south side, of course. I've never been more than a novice climber at best, and Ethan didn't want to kill me.

Point is, Mount Hood's about a five-thousand-foot climb. Up that high, the air's thinner than it is at sea level, which my apartment wasn't all that much above.

Getting my wind back there on the thirteenth landing, I felt like the air was just as thin as it had been that day up atop Mount Hood.

But that was crazy. Couldn't've been. Had to be exhaustion talking.

Once I got as much of my air back as I figured I'd get, I checked out my surroundings. Looked like a regular landing. Still more gray concrete for the walls. Even the ceiling, which should've been a floor lower, looked the same, with one exception.

The overhead light wasn't the single-bar fluorescent I was used to. It was a round lamp, with a shade about two feet wide. Maybe a dozen little bulbs on the other side of that shade, none of them very big or very bright. They even flickered. As though on the other side of that lampshade candles burned, and not lightbulbs.

Why anyone would spend money on lightbulbs that looked like candles was beyond me. But I was pretty darn sure no one came up and lit freaking *candles* to light a landing that wasn't even supposed to be here.

There was the expected door in the expected location, but it had an unexpected look.

We had those steel doors leading into the stairwell on every floor. Fire doors, I think they were called.

But the door here on the thirteenth floor, it was wood. A dark-looking hardwood. Mahogany, maybe. Four panels. With a curved brass handle with a thumb-latch, instead of a knob.

Gotta be honest, here. I almost knocked on that door. As though it could lead straight into one of the condos, when obviously, just like every other floor, it would lead into a hallway, just around the corner from the elevator.

I took the handle in hand. Cold brass, except that, for just a moment, the thumb-latch pulsed warm.

That little pulse made me hesitate, but I opened the latch. When I did, air hissed around the edges of the door. I started to push it open.

And that door did not lead into a hallway.

In fact, the moment the door was open even a crack, I heard music. A rapid, electronic beat overlaid with synthetic horns and high hats. Slow for house music. Fast for hip-hop. Not really loud enough for either. With crunchy guitar chords giving it something like a melody, if that melody allowed for variable spacing in a key signature I didn't recognize. Vaguely middle eastern maybe?

Underneath the music I could hear the sounds of conversation, burbling and swirling as though dozens of people were engaged in pockets of deep discussion.

The smell came next. Pastries. Hot pastries. The richness of their butter and the tangy spices of what had to be some kind of beef filling set my stomach growling.

My stomach had a point. I was hungry from all this exertion, and that glazed donut had been a couple of hours ago. Too long ago to do me any good.

When the door was open wide, what I saw made even less sense.

I knew the floorplan of the condos in the Derringer Building. I'd visited my Gramma and Grandpa Spencer every summer during high school. Since I'd moved in, I'd been inside the condos of a good half-dozen neighbors, whether to drop off some misdelivered mail or for coffee, or a rousing night of boardgames.

If that door on the thirteenth floor led into a condo, it should've led into a tiny foyer. White oak hardwood floor. Likely polar bear white paint for the walls and ceiling. A closet on the left and a half-bath on the right. I should've been able to see the living room through an archway at the end of the foyer, with the kitchen just barely visible off to one side.

Instead, that door opened into a living room unlike any I'd seen anywhere in the building.

First of all, it was big. Big enough to encompass a normal condo's foyer, living room, dining area, and kitchen. And maybe part of the bedrooms. Hard to be sure.

The walls looked like textured plaster, painted olive green below a thick redwood panel that separated the plaster from the maroon wallpaper covered in gold fleur-de-lis. Large cloth-of-gold drapes along the walls. At least two sets per wall. Given their positioning, they couldn't have all been for windows. But what then? Hiding artwork?

More olive green, textured plaster for the vaulted ceiling, with a great big crystal chandelier hanging down. Must've been a hundred little white candles burning in that thing.

The floor ... I didn't know what the floor was. Too smooth for plaster. Too perfect for concrete. It was the color of a pale white oak floor, but without any of the texturing or grooves or...

Oh, hell. I was too busy taking it all in to try to figure out something like that.

I did notice another mahogany door in the center of the far wall, which didn't make sense either. Given the size of the room and the positioning of the stairs, that door had to be leading onto a balcony that didn't exist.

But I knew there was no balcony. And who used solid mahogany for a balcony door anyway?

In the center of the room, four couches faced each other. I didn't know my antiques, but I thought they looked straight out of the courts of one French Louis or another. White wood frames with gold trim, and sewn cushions with flower patterns that matched the flower patterns on the greenish-goldish carpet underneath them.

Little, stick coffee tables in between the couches. Off to one side, a large, mahogany display case stood between two sets of drapes. A silver-clothed buffet table mirrored it on the other wall.

The buffet table was empty, despite the persistent smell of those meaty pastries.

And though I could still hear the soft burbling of conversation under that strange music – not nearly as loud itself as it'd seemed when I opened the door – I couldn't see any people. Or any source of music.

Weirdly enough, it was the lack of people that sent that crawling sensation up the back of my neck. Got my pulse pounding.

I could hear their conversations. I couldn't quite understand their words. Too much interference from other conversations and the music for me to focus on any given voice. And faint as they sounded to me, I could differentiate distances. As though some of the conversations took place near the buffet table, others around the couches, and still others over by the display case.

That was too much.

I mean, maybe somebody was gaslighting me?

No. I walked up a flight of stairs that didn't exist. A flight that took me more effort than *the twelve flights before it combined.*

Whatever was going on here, it wasn't normal.

Only thing I could think, was that all this had to be some kind of ghost shit. Like maybe a special floor with a special condo that only shows up on a special night, once a year.

Like the building equivalent of the Flying Dutchman, or something.

Whatever was going on, I had no intention of getting trapped here in the cocktail party of the damned.

I turned to leave. But the door I'd come through was gone.

I STOOD THERE, ALONE AND TRAPPED INSIDE A ROOM THAT SHOULDN'T exist. Listening to strange electronic music that no one was playing, over the noise of conversations that weren't taking place.

Hell. My stomach was even rumbling at the smell of meat pastries that weren't there.

And now, the door I'd come through – the door that would've led me back to the stairs and my own condo – was gone.

I checked the wall, of course. Patted my fingers along the maroon wallpaper with its gold fleur-de-lis pattern. The single, horizontal panel of redwood that, and the olive green, textured plaster of the wall underneath.

No cracks. No grooves. No sign that the door was still there, but didn't look like a door on this side.

Gone. It was freaking gone.

I just did not want to deal with this. I was hungry. Tired. Muscles in my legs and lower back were all strung out from the effort of ascending that final flight of stairs. Even my feet were kind of stiff and sore inside my sneakers.

All right. Fine. The door was gone? Well, then there had to be some other way out of here and back to the building that I knew.

Maybe ten feet farther along the wall from the place the door should've been was one of those sets of cloth-of-gold drapes. Maybe there was an alcove, or...

I pulled back the drapes, and there was no alcove.

A window. Overlooking a river, among a vast sea of Douglas fir trees...

No. That wasn't right. None of this was right.

I started hyperventilating so bad that the world went red and I got dizzy. I had to lean on the cold glass of the window to keep from falling. I could feel my rapid pulse in my throat. Practically taste it.

I didn't let myself look away, though. Kept my eyes on the view while I tried to rally what was left of my resources.

I could see a mountain in the distance. Snow-capped.

Good. That was good. I was facing east, just like I thought I'd been. And that mountain, that was Mount Hood. Right where it was supposed to be. That meant that the river down below me was the Willamette. Good. I could even see Ross Island there, just to my right. And if I looked a bit to my left...

Yes. There was the Columbia River, coming to meet the Willamette.

This was Oregon. I was still in Oregon, right *about* where I expected to be. Higher up, I was pretty sure, but it was tough to gauge without my normal landmarks.

Yeah. About that last part. The entire fucking Portland metro area was *gone*.

I'd deal with one problem at a time. I had to focus on what I knew.

The sky was purpling in the distance. That was good too. Meant evening was coming on, which meant that the time was about what I expected it to be.

Now. Apart from the entire missing city – well, cities, technically, but one thing at a time – what else was wrong with this picture?

I shouldn't be able to look out a window here and see anything but the inside of the Derringer Building. Well. No. That wasn't quite right. This would be the thirteenth floor, not the twelfth. And as far as I knew, if there *were* a thirteenth floor, it might not be as big as the floors below it.

So if I weren't looking into the building from here, I should still see a good fifty feet of roof between me and the drop-off.

No roof though. And if I pressed my forehead to the glass, I could see...

Oh, son of a bitch. There was no building below me either.

You know, looking back that probably should've messed me up. But it'd been one shock after another for long enough that not seeing anything below that window except hundreds of feet of air above the tips of those fir trees down there just made me feel even more tired.

Why, oh why, had I taken those mystery stairs?

I forced a deep breath in and out, discovering as I did that my shoulders had tightened up like the concrete of those stairs.

All right. I knew there was nothing on the coffee tables behind me. I knew there was nothing on the buffet table either. Mind you, I could still hear that music, and those conversations, and I could still smell those maddeningly seductive meat pies.

But the display case. I hadn't actually looked at what was behind the glass. Maybe there was something on one of the shelves that could help me. Or maybe something in the base. In a drawer, perhaps.

Wait. That door on the other side of the room.

I turned away from the window and the ocean of fir trees.

Yep. That door on the other side was still there. I glanced to my left, hoping the door I'd come through had reappeared, but it hadn't.

Maybe that was a good thing, though. Maybe that door on the other wall, maybe it was the door home.

No, that didn't make any more sense to me than it probably does to you. But after everything else, why *shouldn't* the doors be playing musical chairs?

That was an image I didn't need. I started making this breathless, chuckling sound that felt all too ready to turn into hysterical laughter.

I reined it in, holding it to a steady, staccato chuckle no louder than those conversations, as I made my way across the floor. I half-expected to bump into one of those people I could hear but not see. Didn't happen. I made it all the way to that other door.

The door was locked.

Wait.

This door had a doorknob. Not a handle. Yes, it was still brass, but it was a doorknob. What did that mean?

It meant that maybe I should've studied more history, because I was drawing a blank. For all I knew, every French court since Louis XII had had doorknobs.

That was what finally broke the dam on the hysterical laughter.

I was nowhere near France. I was hundreds of feet in the air – maybe a thousand or more – and there was nothing between me and a forest full of trees except the floor of the room I stood in.

A doorknob was the least of my worries.

The hysterical laughter actually felt kind of good. Gave all my muscles a different sort of workout, and got me lightheaded. Gave everything a coat of surreality.

I was just starting to enjoy it when I heard a voice.

"You're not supposed to be here."

It was a woman's voice. Soft in timbre, but loud with surprise. And the moment I heard it, I realized I wasn't hearing any music, or those background conversations.

Shock stopped my laughter.

I whipped around to see who spoke, but I was too lightheaded and breathless from uncontrolled spasms of laughter. I tripped over my own feet and landed hard on that floor. That strange floor. Looked hard as marble, but it felt no harder than hardwood.

I saw the speaker, though. And she was a woman, all right. Maybe five feet tall, or about that, which made her a foot shorter than me. When I was standing.

She had blonde hair in a pixie cut, black framed glasses, and was wearing a bulky white jumpsuit that looked like a fabric made from plastics. It was covered in pockets, and she wore the legs tucked into white boots that looked to have been made from the same material. Her gloves looked like blue nitrile, though.

"Hi," I said, working my way back to my feet over the protests of my muscles. They were tired enough that any lying down felt like a better option to them than more work. I tried smiling though, and I hope it worked. "Didn't mean to intrude."

"Who are you?" she asked, frowning as she looked me over. "Your clothing..." She shook her head. "No. First things first. Who are you?"

"Brandon Spencer," I said. "And you are?"

"The one asking the questions right now," she said, and pulled what looked like a small sheet of glass out of her breast pocket. She flicked it with a finger, and it came to life, displaying graphics I couldn't make sense of from where I now stood.

"Oh, come on," I said, smiling to try to make it sound as though we were on the same side, even though I had even less idea now of what was going on than I had a moment ago. "You can at least tell me your name."

"Might not be safe," she said absently, frowning at the readouts she was getting one what had to be a sensor of some sort. Or maybe a phone more advanced than anything I'd ever seen.

She flicked her finger up across the screen and looked at me like I was a science experiment.

"Cottons," she muttered, "simple synthetics, rubber in the shoes, metal in the keys. Hello." Where she was looking made me flush for a moment, until I realized she was looking a few inches down and to the right, at the cargo pants pocket where I kept my phone. "*That's* your best tech?"

"Hey," I said. "It's this year's model."

"Is it?" She nodded. Swiped the screen left a few times, then up, right, and down a few more. All while looking me over in that detached, studious way. "All right. So you're from the year 2020? The ... United States of America? What was it then? Oregon?"

I didn't answer. I was too busy paling and feeling my mouth get dry.

She didn't wait for me to answer anyway. Nodded as though I had.

"How did you get here?"

"No," I said.

That made her blink and actually look at me, instead of whatever heads-up display she had overlain me with.

"Excuse me?" she said.

"I said, 'no.'" I shook my head and crossed my arms. "I didn't want to come here. I don't know where I am. And you just show up, expecting me to answer all your questions when, far as I'm concerned, you've abducted me? Not gonna happen."

"Abducted you?" she asked, astonished. "How do you figure—"

"You've absconded with me in this ... whatever it is, for your own reasons, and you won't even tell me your name."

"Look," she said, and I knew that exasperation well. I'd worked in tech support for too long, not to recognize the look of a tech who feels put-upon. "I'm not going to tell you my name, because I'm hoping to be able to get you home. *Your* home. The less you know, the more likely I can do that."

Here's the thing about working I.T. You get to know all the little tells of I.T. workers. And this woman, she was telling me half-truths to make her life easier.

I had no reason to make her life easier. In fact, I suspected that if anything bad happened to me during her shift, *she'd* be stuck with paperwork at the best, a reprimand or firing at the worst.

So I pushed.

I pointed to the window and its amazing forest view.

"That," I said dramatically, "is not the future. So don't try to hand me some bunk about time travel."

"You don't want to know. Believe me."

"Yeah?" I shook my head and crossed my arms again. "Well I don't want my mind to snap like a twig, either. And you heard my laughter when you showed up. I'm teetering on the brink. You help me make sense of this or it won't matter where you send me, unless it has rubber walls."

Truthfully, I was further now from snapping than I'd been before she showed up. The familiarity of an I.T. situation gave me a handle for my sanity to cling to.

But I must've sold it with the comment about that laughter. She sighed the sigh I'd sighed myself more than a half-dozen times that week alone.

"All right," she said, and sighed again. "You're not in the future. Or the past. This room, it's outside of time."

"That's not possible."

"You keep thinking that." She rolled her eyes. "That'll help you stay sane."

"But..." I started, pointing out the window where, down below, it was obvious that wind was blowing through the trees.

"That window shows a very specific time frame," she said, then added quickly, "not telling you when." She nodded at another set of curtains. "In fact, each set of curtains will show a different time frame for this location. I don't recommend sightseeing, though."

"No," I said in complete honesty, "my psyche is fragile enough, thank you."

Exaggeration? Maybe. But my heart was pounding again at the implications of what this woman was telling me. Viewing windows to different time frames? An entire, self-contained room outside of time itself?

But to this woman the implications were old hat. Because she continued right along toward her goal.

"Good. Now. I need to know when you came from, and how you got here, if we're going to have any chance of sending you home." She shook her head, fiddled with her display and muttered, "Isn't exactly someplace you can stumble into."

"But that's exactly what I *did* do."

I explained about the Derringer Building, the unexpected staircase, the trek up, and finally the door that led in. I was just starting in on the music, the conversations and the phantom pastries when she spoke over me.

"No." She shook her head. "Crap! That must've been echoes the staff party last weekend. Meat pies, you said, right? Do you know what hovena is?"

I shook my head.

"Better not tell you then," she said, talking to herself and fiddling more with what I'd now decided was her control unit for whatever heads up display she could just see with her own eyes.

She shook her head, mumbling about echoes and resonances the way I bitched at work about Wi-Fi issues and botched DNS settings.

"Unfortunately," she said, tapping her control unit as though it was giving her information that backed up what she was saying, "what you said is impossible. There's no route here from the Derringer Building ever. Much less in 2020."

She frowned and shook her head while my stomach tried to sink down through the floor and go free-falling.

"Now," she said, giving me a stern look, "if you don't tell me the truth, we can't help each other."

"I'm telling you the truth," I said through a sigh that darn near deflated me. I shrugged. "I can show you my driver's license. Prove my address one floor down. More or less. Beyond that—"

"Toss it here," she said, holding out a blue hand.

I frowned at her implication that we shouldn't come close enough together for me to just hand it to her, but realized that might be smarter. I didn't know when she was from, and had no idea what germs she carried that I might not be immune to. Or, for that matter, what germs *I* carried that people in her time might no longer be immune to.

I tossed her the driver's license and she caught it neatly. Passed it through the air in front of her control unit. Tossed it back to me. Fiddled with her control unit while staring at the air above her device.

"Well," she said, and her frown had spread to crease lines

between her eyebrows, "this confirms when and where you're from. But how you got here makes no sense."

"You're telling me," I said. "So how do we get me home?"

"Tell me again," she said, and her focus now was sharp. A troubleshooting focus if I'd ever seen one. Made me feel as though I were working with a colleague, rather than trusting a stranger to get me out of a mess I could never have conceived of on my own.

I went slowly through everything I'd done since leaving work. How I hopped on the MAX light rail train in Beaverton and ridden it downtown while reading a fantasy novel on my phone. Even told her the name of the author and the title of the book, in case they mattered.

The straight-line route I'd followed from the light rail station to the Derringer Building. When I mentioned the electronic key card I used to open the door, her eyes got wide.

"Electronic key card? You didn't mention that before."

"It didn't have anything to do with the stairwell."

I could practically hear her counting to ten in her head, to avoid yelling at me. I didn't make her ask to see the key card. Just tossed it to her.

She passed it in front of her control unit as she had my driver's license, then tossed the key card back to me.

"What will that do?" I asked, as interrupting the way she mumbled to herself while flicking and swirling her finger to manipulate her control unit.

"Think of it as the difference between using an industrial-strength magnet to search for a needle in a haystack, rather than doing it by hand. *Here* we go."

"What?"

She frowned. Looked down as though she could see my building underneath her. Double-checked something. Sighed and shook her head.

"What?" I asked, exasperated.

"Huh. When you said you lived in the Derringer Building, I thought you meant the *Derringer* Building."

"Come again?"

"It's nothing. Turns out there were two. That's all. The Derringer Building was rebuilt after the fire of..." She gave me a sharp look. "After a fire you'll never have to worry about. The building I was thinking of isn't important anyway. Yours was the one before the fire."

Her face scrunched up in irritation. "Our records from before that fire are spotty in this part of Portland. The most recent photo I can find comes from..." – another frowning glance – "let's just say some-time in your lifetime. But there's a gap between the timestamp of that photo and the fire."

"They built up? Added more floors?"

"Must've."

I shook my head. "But this is a condo. They couldn't do it without permission from the associa..."

I let that thought trail off while realization set in. By the by, not a lot of fun doing that kind of thinking while someone is visibly staring at you, trying to will you to come to the answer on your own.

"Population density," I said. "Portland's growing too fast. They need housing. Might be a city ordinance—"

"And that's enough of that," she said, trying to snap her fingers and failing because of the powder in her nitrile gloves. "Point is, there's a way. But it wasn't done in 2020. So why did you find that staircase? And how did you get here?"

"You already answered that," I said. "Resonance. Temporal resonance."

"But that wouldn't account for the staircase."

"Yes, it would," I said, starting to feel that good flutter in my stom-ach. The one that told me I was solving a problem. "You put a wall," – I pointed to the wall I came through – "where there just happened to have been a wall once. At a time when there was a stairwell from the twelfth to thirteenth floors. A time where there'd been a door right here."

I walked over and patted that wall at what I thought was the spot I came through.

"You think it was signal decay?" she said, frowning. Then shook her head and frowned at me. "What the hell do you know about temporal resonance?"

"Specifically? Nothing," I said. "But I understand resonance as a concept. And I know how echoes work, both in the sound sense and in the network sense. Just extrapolating from there."

She was checking something on her control unit, so I kept talking.

"So," I said. "If I'm right, then you tried to put this room where there'd never been anything before, so it couldn't possibly interact with anything *inside* time. But this building must've been built up without your team knowing. So when the echo problem creeped in, it resonated with a wall that'd been there in your past and my future, which connected the echo with just enough spacetime around it to encompass the stairs when I just happened to be in a position to interact."

My turn to frown, as a cold realization spread through me.

If this was true, and the resonance problem was fixed – I noted all too well the lack of music, background conversations, and meat pastry smells – then I was stuck here outside time.

"Hah!" she said, holding up her control unit triumphantly. "Found it. Blueprints and building permits. Exactly one set had survived the—"

She gave me a quick look.

"I already know about the fire," I said, feeling hope welling in my chest that she'd found some kind of solution. "Remember? You said I wouldn't have to worry about it."

She tapped herself three times on the forehead, as though chiding herself for admitting potentially time-changing information.

"Look," she started, but I cut her off.

"I'm not going to say anything," I said. "Please. I'm going to warn people about a huge fire coming when? Someday? Even if I tried – and anyone believed me, which we both know they wouldn't – who'd give it precedence over worries about a future earthquake? A much bigger concern in this area, believe me."

She gave me a grudging nod, and continued. "The set owned by the ... current owners of the building at the time of the fire. They lived in another state, and didn't register them properly with..."

She shook her head. Snorted a laugh.

"Listen to me, talking to you like a colleague and not a victim of circumstance."

"I don't mind," I said. "I do I.T. myself."

"I know," she said, and didn't explain that part as she continued. "Point is, you're right. There'd been a building right in this spot in my past and your future. And when those slackers at the party last weekend failed to clean up after themselves, you got caught in the echoes."

Fear clenched my stomach hard enough to make me bend over. "So I'm stuck here?"

She actually laughed at that one.

"Come on," she said. "I thought you said you worked I.T."

Hope warred with fear in my guts. I forced a tentative smile.

"You mean," I said, slowly, "you can recreate the resonance?"

"I marked the settings before fixing them. I can just reset them."

She did so, while I watched the wall I'd come through, and fear won out over hope in my chest because of what I didn't see.

"The door," I said. "The one I came through. It's not there."

THE FUTURE I.T. TECH AND I STARED AT EACH OTHER ACROSS A ROOM that look far more archaic to me than futuristic. I mean, why, in the future, would they use old French court furnishings and plaster walls? And that wallpaper with the fleur-de-lis? What was that about anyway?

She looked over at the olive-green plaster where there was no door for me to leave through.

"We didn't put a door there," she said.

"Obviously," I said.

"So as soon as you closed the door behind you..."

"I didn't," I said. "Must've had one of those pneumatic closers. I didn't notice, but the other floors all have them." My turn to frown. "That door wasn't steel like the others, by the way. It was—"

"You might as well forget what that door was made of," she said absently, while playing with her clear control unit, making colors and shapes I couldn't interpret. "You'll never see it in your lifetime anyway."

I was pretty sure it'd been mahogany. And I wasn't going to forget, just to be obstinate.

"What about that other door?" I said, pointing across the big room at the one outside door the room had. "It's mahogany too."

Realization carbonated its way through me, making my arms and legs tremble.

"Four panels," I said. "Just like the other. Except..."

"Except what?" she sounded urgent now. Encouraging.

"Except that it has a knob, and the door I came through—"

"A handle with a thumb latch!" She was bouncing in excitement now. "Did you feel anything odd about that thumb-latch?"

Hope came roaring back through me.

"Yes! It felt warm when my thumb first touched it."

"Yes!" she said, thrusting a fist in the air. "It *was* that door. Had to have reverberated..."

I think she said something else about pings and decay rates, but I didn't catch the rest of what she said. She mumbled to herself while her fingers played that control unit like a concert virtuoso on a keyboard.

A moment later, the door I came through showed up again.

"Go!" she said. "And good luck."

I turned the knob and pulled the door open.

There was the landing again. With the strange pseudo-candelabra hanging down above.

I didn't question it. I hustled for the stairs and started down.

Now, all the excitement in the room outside time had made me forget just how tired I was. But trying to go down those steps again brought all of that screaming back.

My poor, exhausted legs and feet started complaining before I got three steps down that thirteenth flight. My lower back started registering its own issues a step later.

I...

All right. This is a little weird to admit. But when my big brother found out I'd started running, back in college, he sent me a tape of United States Navy SEAL cadences, to run to.

On my way down that thirteenth flight of stairs, I found myself chanting cadences under my breath. About a dog named Blue who wanted to be a SEAL. About the Chief Petty Officer fighting Superman. All kinds of things I never thought about in my daily life.

But those cadences did their job. They gave me focus. Regulated my breathing. Most important, they helped me ignore the growing soreness in my quads and hammies and calves and arches.

I made it down that nigh-infinite single flight of stairs – trying not to bitch at how the temporal I.T. tech had failed to tell me *why* that flight of stairs was so exhausting – and collapsed in a sweaty heap on the gray concrete of the twelfth floor landing.

Never thought I'd feel so glad to smell that awful, fermented concrete odor.

I watched those phantom stairs fade away, and resolved to never again take any staircase that wasn't supposed to be there.

PARADOX. LOST.

PARADOX. LOST.

It was all my fault. Or it will be. I'm not sure when I am anymore.

Which means I have to stick to now. Right now. For as long as I have.

I'm standing in wild grass that reaches to my waist and smells dry, even though it's still on the green side of yellow. Clean, strong wind cooling off the hot sun. Cleaner than the air I remember from that conference in the Swiss Alps.

The sky is a rich, royal blue, with thunderheads the size of mountains coming in from the . . . south? . . . over that huge forest full of trees that are each wider than my house. Evergreens, but I don't recognize the type.

Worse, I'm not sure exactly *where* I am. American southwest, or Europe maybe. Definitely not Haiti, anyway. That means the last shift didn't just take me through time. It took me through space. The collapse is happening faster than I—

What the hell was that? Sounded like fifteen tons of rusted steel being torn in half. So loud my ears are still buzzing.

Wait. That shadow. I look up, shielding my eyes against the harsh morning (or is it afternoon?) sun.

Dear God in heaven. I must be in the Triassic or Cretaceous period, because that can only be a pterosaur. Skin like green leather. Wingspan like a jumbo jet. Too big, though. No records of them growing that big. Beak full of teeth bigger than my six-foot frame.

It sees me.

It's diving.

Guess I'm not allowed to die yet. Probably have to die last. Or something.

My simple t-shirt and jeans aren't enough for this cold winter air. I'm shivering as I notice I'm on the last car in a New York subway line. Empty, except for a young couple in the back. Something familiar about this. The yellow light. The peeling ads for the *CATS* revival. The smell of spilled bourbon, old urine and . . . bubble gum? Why does that tickle the back of my memory?

The passenger straps. They've got that powdery smell like stale bubble gum. Something to do with that "self-cleaning" stretchy-strong yellow fabric they're made from. New York installed those things around 2020, when I was in high school.

That's it! That's me in the back, with Rashonda Jenkins. She used to tease me that I was the only guy in our high school with darker skin than hers. Oh, God, I still had that fade. It's junior year—2021—and I'm about to kiss her for the first time, on our way back from watching the Knicks lose to the Trail Blazers. Rashonda, with those cheerleader curves and that hint of lilac perfume that drove me wild—

"What are you staring at?"

Teenage me on my feet now, yelling at current me. Puffed up to impress my girl. Cocky half-grin on my face because no one messed with someone my size. I've lost a lot of weight since then. Some because I gave up football, but more because I gave up double cheeseburgers with everything.

I didn't yell at anyone that night, though. I remember it clearly. I'd found an empty car toward the back where I could be alone with Rashonda, and we got so involved in each other that we missed our stop and ended up in Queens. Laughed about it the whole time we were dating.

That memory isn't changing. What happened to me happened, even though it's different than what's happening to teenage me right this second.

Another paradox. Another layer collapsing.

"N-Nothing," I say to my younger self. I sound scared, but it's just the cold. Truth is, this is all happening too fast for me to really be sure what I'm feeling. Anyway, I raise my hands in surrender. Maybe if I get out of here now, I can get them back on track. Slow down the—

"He related to you, baby?" asks Rashonda. "'Cause I swear he's got that little twist to his nose, just like you. And his eyes."

I turn away before I make things worse, wedge the sticky door open, and push into the next car. But the damage is done. A glance through the streaked, dirty glass of the door shows they're talking about me.

Even if my first kiss with Rashonda dominated my memories of the night, there's no way an encounter like this would have faded from my recollection.

If it happened. But it didn't.

Except that it's happening right now. Which is the whole problem.

Maybe—I can get a message to myself. Time-delayed delivery. Keep me from inventing the—

I almost laugh when I see him appear in the middle of the aisle in front of me, between the middle-aged woman with her nose buried in a book and the pseudosuit guy talking loudly on his phone.

The new arrival is so out of place I can't help wanting to ask, "Who's the reject from Historic Jamestown?" Except I've got that sinking feeling in my gut, the one that makes me wish for the third time since this started that my most recent meal had been something other than cafeteria lunchtime lasagna. There can't be any of it left by now, but it still somehow feels like lead in my stomach.

The new arrival's got the powdered wig and face and the bright blue outfit with gold trim that screams both Colonial period and money. Can't even see a scuff mark on those tall brown shoes. The kind of guy who probably owned—owns—slaves, which I admit makes me feel just little less sympathy for the abject terror on his face. His eyes are wide and trying to see everything at once. His nose wrinkles likes it's trying to suck itself into his face to get away from the smells of the New York subway system.

He starts spinning in circles, trying to back away from everything at once, one hand scrambling for a handkerchief.

I don't need this right now. I've got enough of my own fear to deal with. Because his presence here assures me I'm not the only one unstuck in time.

I was right. It's all collapsing.

Colonial guy collapses too. Passes out right there.

Damn it. I can't just ignore this like the two proper New Yorkers, reading and yelling into a phone respectively. After all, it's my fault the poor bastard's here.

I kneel next to him. Pat his pale, powdered cheek gently. "Hey, buddy. You in there?"

Whoa.

Now I'm standing on a colorless, transparent bridge, three meters wide and no more than two meters above an ocean. (Wasn't I kneeling a moment ago? Or hasn't that happened yet?) Cold sea air in my nose. Wind whipping me in three directions at once, each carrying cold spray with it. Ahead of me are a series of translucent towers of what looks like the same material, but done in gentle sea colors like coral. They start barely ten meters from me, and they go up and up and up . . .

Vertigo drops me back to my knees, makes me slap the bridge

with my hands, but it's solid. Sure. Smooth like glass, but not quite right. Too . . . dense feeling. I knock on it, and it *thump*s instead of ringing.

Wait. It should be wet. Why isn't it wet?

My scientific curiosity overrules other immediate concerns. I crouch way down and watch for a moment as the constantly shifting wind sprays the bridge (and me, which is not helping my shivering body cope). Water hits the surface of the bridge, then slides right off to the sea below it.

Looks frictionless, but it can't be. I would have slid off the moment I arrived. I stand and take a step forward. The bridge feels solid and steady underfoot. I try to slide my sneaker forward and back, but the bridge doesn't let me.

Water slides off, but my shoe won't budge unless I lift it. Must be a designed molecule of some sort. We don't even have that in 2046, which means . . .

This is the future. A future I won't live to see. If you don't count my presence here right now.

But I do have right now. Until the collapse takes me away again.

I start running toward the towers, keeping my eyes low to avoid another bout of vertigo. No people yet, but they have to be here somewhere.

My whole presence here is another paradox. If I lived to see this, I should be considerably older than forty-one. But I don't know when this is. There's a reasonable chance that the me who lived to see this year didn't. Died somewhere along the way.

Halfway to the towers, I hear a whirring hum above me. I look up—

—and fall flat on my back on the hard, unforgiving surface of the bridge.

The sight is worth it.

Spaceships.

I don't mean those little space capsules we all know and love. I mean giant, aerodynamic tubes of greenish translucence that must be big enough to carry thousands of people. Hundreds of thousands, maybe. Maybe millions, across the dozen or so ships I can see.

The near end of the tubes glows pinkish, and each one streaks out into the skies. Seconds later the whirring hum is replaced by a series of sucking *pops*, followed by the distant *boom*s of the sound barrier's complaint.

Those ships had to be bigger than I thought if I could hear them break the sound barrier from that far away. I try to play with the math in my head as I stand and start toward the towers again.

Still no sign of people.

A distant sound in the skies behind me, like . . . torn metal.

I turn and see the pterosaur again. All right, maybe it's not the same one, but it's huge and green and maybe I'm reading something into this, but it looks mad at being deprived of its earlier meal. At least it's further away this time. I have time to run toward those towers and—

Now this place I know. The smooth, tan, polymer flooring. The lemon chemical smell of the cleaner I love so much. The tankless water heater and microfurnace. The camping gear neatly folded on the racks of one wall, waiting for my summer "adventures."

And the scene of the crime—the work bench with all the high-end tech toys I convinced the company I *needed* to have. Because when you have five doctorates and no life, you pretty much work even when you're off the clock.

This is my garage. And I have a sneaking suspicion the date is April 2nd, 2046. Yep, there I am now, right on schedule, pulling into the garage in my collapsedan. Home from the lab, with a sack of takeout orange chicken, rice, and eggrolls that will sit on one end of the work bench and get cold while I fiddle with the worst idea in human history.

I duck behind the camping equipment while 2046 me collapses the car and activates the ceiling dock to float it up and out of the way.

2046 me then sets the sack of food on the work bench and goes into the house to change out of the company-mandated suit and into what I'm wearing now. My stomach rumbles at the thought of that food. I hadn't eaten in five hours when I got home that day—today—and I have no idea how much time has sort-of passed for me since then. I know I spent at least five hours working that night, before I took the jump that started it all.

All because of what I read on the 'nets that day. That paper from the Bangladesh Hadron Collider. Tachyons. They were real, and they went faster than light. The article included measurements. Some calculations. Lots more theory.

I should have been excited at the prospect of more research, like everyone else. So much to learn. The possibility of distant space travel within a generation or two.

Discoveries like that don't happen every day.

But I didn't want to develop space travel. No, I wanted to play H. G. Wells.

Well, Cedric, let's see how well you invent *without* all that fancy equipment.

I toss every piece of high-end tech right under the car dock. The computer, the Variable Meter™, the portacollider, and all the rest. Then I go to the breaker panel under the microfurnace and kill the garage power.

The collapsedan drops its half-ton of unforgiving alloys fifteen feet onto equipment that cost more than I could make in five years, even if I owned *all* of my patents.

The crash makes me smile.

Wait. I'm still here.

Did I stop it? If I did that, instead of inventing the time sequencer, I might be standing exactly where I am, exactly when I am.

Hopeful relief floods out of me in a shuddering breath. My shoulders are still hunched, expecting the other shoe to drop, but after a few seconds I decide this must have worked.

I fling both fists, in the air in triumph with a whoop I haven't let out since my football days.

I grab a couple of eggrolls, stuff one in my mouth and turn toward the door into the house.

A door that opens. 2046 me, dressed just like I am now. He yells, "What the hell is—"

Then he sees me. Gets our look of recognition, like he put it all together in his head every bit as fast as I like to think I would have in his shoes.

"You're here to stop me," 2046 me says.

"I tried," I say.

STICKY HEAT, AND AIR THAT SMELLS LIKE DIESEL, AND DIRT, AND FISH, and rice, and sweaty people. Lots of them, all around me. Hundreds or more, dressed in the lightest clothing they can manage. White shirts with rolled-up sleeves over old jeans, also rolled-up to varying degrees. Women in thin dresses, white and yellow. Angry men and women in red shirts and red dresses, like the color is a statement.

Some suits and ties in the crowd, mostly worn by white people who look like reporters. Which makes sense, because the business-people would be watching from a safe distance, whether local or American.

And the police, of course, are everywhere, to provide "security."

Everyone is spread out over the passable asphalt and concrete of the street in front of the house of François Duvalier. Papa Doc. Waiting to hear the President of Haiti speak.

It's April, 1961. I may already be somewhere in the crowd, with that old hand-me-down .38.

It's the oldest question in the time travel game. "Would you try to kill Hitler, and could you succeed?" I've been involved in 'net debates about it since I was a kid. So, naturally, when I figured out how to make the time sequencer work, I wondered if I should do it. *Could* do it.

But Hitler, he must have changed more than a billion lives. Not just all the people exterminated in camps or killed during the war, but look at the long-term effects of the war. Economically. Sociologically. More than a century later, I could argue that we're still seeing the results.

So killing him would change a whole lot. But why go for the big target right away? Why not test the ripples of a smaller target first?

Why not take out the man who killed thousands and ground Haiti under his heel for years? The man who drove my family out of their homes. Made my ancestors flee in the night like criminals because of their politics.

And why not take him out just before he really started consolidating his power?

1961. That's when it all started to go *really* wrong under Duvalier. So that was the perfect time to try to save a whole bunch of lives.

And there I am now, trying to ignore the weight of the .38 at the base of my spine. To pretend it isn't there, while I try to get close enough for the shot.

I wonder if I can stop me? Maybe that's why I'm here. Stop me from shooting the bullet that took Papa Doc through the forehead and started the whole collapse.

Maybe I can—

Not that pterosaur again. That awful, screaming roar.

The crowd panics. I get knocked off my feet while people are screaming all around me. Shoving. Running. Stomping on my side, back, legs as they go. It's all I can do to huddle up and protect my head.

Gunshots now. The police firing on the giant dinosaur.

Someone grabbing my shoulder. Pulling me up.

It's me. 1961 me. Recognizing me. Shock. Panic.

"It would have been a good shot," I say, but my words are drowned out by a sudden humming whirr. The spaceships. Filling the sky. Thousands.

People around me vanish. Replaced by others. Knights on horseback. Samurai. Zulu warriors. Egyptian priests. Ancient Chinese farmers. Coming and going in the blink of an eye.

An Apatosaurus stomps along a wide field where the Caribbean

Sea should be, chased by a crude gray German tank from . . . World War I, I think?

The sun is moving backwards now, passing itself in the sky while three moons circle overhead. My patch of asphalt is in the mountains now, surrounded by snow and at least one yeti. I don't feel cold, but for some reason it doesn't worry me.

I'm hearing my father yelling encouragements on the football field. Yelling for me to spin away from linebackers. At the same time, I'm hearing the test proctor giving instructions for my GRE. And President Eisenhower giving a speech I wasn't alive to hear. And something that sounds like Greek. And my grandmother cooing about how big and strong I'm getting already, and such a grip!

I can feel her squeeze my finger. And that right cross to the breadbasket Jimmy Montrose gave me for making fun of his car. And the bone-deep drain of the third full day of practice after that loss we should have won. And the hang on my neck of the Nobel medal for my work with tachyons (wait, I don't remember that).

But nothing waits right now. Everything happens at once.

I'm tasting Mom's *pwason_fri*, with the red snapper fried up perfectly and that touch of habanero. And peanut butter and jelly on rye instead of the peanut butter and honey on whole wheat that were a staple of my school days. And that barbecued shrimp I had in New Orleans that time. And seawater. And . . . cordite? And the goose liver paté Shirley made me. (Who's Shirley?)

Nothing blending. All these things independently, yet together. Some from my own life. Some from my almost-was future. Some . . . not mine at all, but still reaching me now.

I'm smelling my mother's milk. And the high school locker room. And the fresh grass after I've been tackled. And camel dung. And the burnt hair from that dorm party that went wrong.

And Rashonda's lilac perfume.

And now everything's gone black.

SIGN UP FOR STEFON'S NEWSLETTER

Stefon loves to keep in touch with his readers, and loves to keep you reading. The best way for him to do both is for you to sign up for his newsletter.

Sign up at http://www.stefonmears.com/join

If you sign up for Stefon's newsletter, you get...

- Monthly updates about his publishing and travel schedules
- His latest news, in brief, and answers to reader questions
- A free short story for signing up
- List-only offers and occasional specials
- Plus a free short story every month!

ABOUT THE AUTHOR

If Stefon Mears could stop time, he'd get even more reading done. Stefon has more than thirty books to his credit, and he never stops writing. He earned his M.F.A. in Creative Writing from N.I.L.A., and his B.A. in Religious Studies (double emphasis in Ritual and Mythology) from U.C. Berkeley. He's a lifelong gamer and fantasy fan. Stefon lives in Portland, Oregon, with his wife and three cats.

Look for Stefon online:
www.stefonmears.com
himself@stefonmears.com

www.ingramcontent.com/pod-product-compliance
Lightning Source LLC
Chambersburg PA
CBHW030755200726
48288CB00004B/1186